The   *the*
night. (*had*
a job t   *ried*
about l   *logy*
projects to look forward to. Dinosaurs were beckoning. It was time to get her life back on track, and Jack wasn't part of it. He was just a fascinating diversion. She needed a man in a civilized suit, a man with a haircut, and a bank account.

Camouflage had become a habit with each of them, he with his shaggy hair and rough clothes, she with her temper and I-don't-give-a-damn attitude. They had forgotten that nature makes its own rules and has its own solutions.

The Author

Marguérite Turnley lives in Australia on a six-acre paddock. She shares her life with three children, a long suffering husband, two neurotic dogs and a fluffy cat who sleeps next to her computer and sheds fur on the mouse pad. A Gemini, Marguérite has a dual personality. She paints landscapes, some with acrylic paint, some with words. She loves to make people laugh.

*To Sandra, Ruth, Julie, Sue and Margaret,
thanks for the unfailing support and encouragement.*

Thanks to my family for everything.

*Special thanks to my own primal man for giving me
a computer and showing me how it works.*

Marguérite Turnley

Primal Man

Published in the USA in 2006

Copyright © by Marguérite Turnley 2006

SALTWATER PRESS
Post Office Box 535
Merrylands NSW 2160
Australia

ISBN
1-74062-027-5

The outback road lay hot and hard in front of her, devoid of human life. The covered jeep Cassie Travis was driving slowed and stopped without warning. "What the hell is wrong now?" she muttered, pumping the accelerator. Nothing happened. There was something seriously wrong with the vehicle. The fuel gage was showing empty but she'd already gassed it up twice in the last hour with the spare cans she was carrying.

Cassie flipped her cell phone open and swore vividly. Nothing. Back home in Nevada at least she'd have cell phone reception. Here in Australia even steering wheels were on the wrong side.

She had decided, at an early age, never to rely on anyone but herself. Being independent was essential. She refused to rely on her family to bail her out of trouble. Her brothers would be saying 'I told you so' right about now. They'd probably send her an airline ticket home just to get her back under their control. No way was that going to happen. She was out of their jurisdiction and she planned to stay that way.

Crawling under the vehicle was never a pleasant job, but since there was no garage in sight on the deserted road, she decided she'd better get on with it. Lying down on the hot dirt track, Cassie wriggled under the jeep, inspecting it carefully. Her cotton shirt and jeans were no protection against the hard stones and coarse red sand. There was a strong smell of gasoline. When she discovered where it was coming from, a fresh burst of descriptive language issued forth, something about the reproductive abilities of metal. You can learn a lot at an Aussie pub she thought, trying to regain her sense of humor as she twisted and turned under the jeep, wishing she had a phone that worked. Just like home, Aussies drink their beer cold. Pity I don't have a can of Fosters Lager to cool off.

The fuel tank had been ruptured. It had to be that rock she had driven over in the dry creek bed. The jeep had crunched down to its springs, but had not seemed to be damaged. Cassie was not happy.

As she wormed her way out from under the vehicle, she wondered what she was going to do. "This is all I need," she said, standing up and looking around. "Damn!"

The landscape stretched for miles into the distant plains of the Simpson Desert, sunlight on the saltpans giving a luminous glow. The few trees were hardly big enough to shade the lizard she could see, stepping across the road as if its feet were burning. They probably are, she thought, but at least he knows where he's going.

Interspersed were large pale-barked trees she had been told were ghost gums. They look like creepy lone sentinels she thought, and knew now how that felt. Being alone right now was not a good place to be.

Cassie wished she had heeded the words of the gas station guy in Alice Springs. He had warned her about traveling in the desert alone but, confident of her survival skills, she hadn't taken his advice. Buying several extra cans of gasoline as well wouldn't have broken the bank. She had already used the two cans she had and was hoping to reach the next garage on the map before she ran out. Not that it would have done any good to buy more. What she needed right now was something to plug the hole in the tank.

Hot, dry air parched her throat and she thought, as she drank from her water bottle, what I wouldn't give for a long, icy-cold beer.

Hills arose blue and purple in the distance as they became the East Mac Donnell Ranges. Red iron ore, shadowed with black and purple, colored closer outcrops of rock as they shone in the afternoon sunlight. To the south was more desert country, its starkness softened by scrub grass and a few gaunt trees. There wasn't a vehicle, house or person within view. Even the kangaroos and wombats had gone to ground. In fact, there was barely a road, just a rough dirt track with straggly patches of grass and weeds.

The town of Jasper Creek was another hour or two hour away by car. The side trip she'd taken, to view an interesting rock formation at the foot of Mt. Brassey, had proven to be a major error in judgment. To walk the distance back to the Plenty Highway would take more food and water than Cassie had brought with her.

She was on a camping trip in the eastern foothills of the Harte Range, having high hopes of visiting an archaeological dig at Alcoota, northeast from Alice Springs. A letter of introduction from a professor at the University of Nevada to people already on site was in her pocketbook. She'd met him back in the States and he'd encouraged her to come to Australia on the chance of a dig in the desert, the chance of a lifetime.

It was something she had dreamed of ever since she was a teenager traveling with her brothers. She'd had to prove herself then, and circumstances hadn't changed. Determination to succeed was part of her now.

Her plans were dashed as she looked at the broken

down jeep. Dreams were a fine thing but they weren't much good if you were stuck without transport.

Cassie ran her hands through her hair in disgust; perspiration and dust gathered on her face, giving her a taste of what was to come. She was only twenty-three, but was familiar with wilderness areas, having spent much of her childhood camping out. Her vacations were usually spent backpacking, looking for relics of the past.

Prehistoric bones of unknown origin and anything that would point the way to the ancient history of the American continent were of interest to her. Australia drew her in the same way. Both countries had secrets she wanted to discover.

Some people said she was obsessive, but she kept on looking, hoping for a find that would shake the experts out of their complacency. The center of Australia was once covered by water; Cassie was looking for evidence of prehistoric sea creatures as well as land dwellers. She'd even read about a giant, meat-eating duck with teeth called a *bulockornis planei* stomping around the Northern Territory. That had been a really special find. If she found something, no one would dare call her obsessive. The word they'd use would be 'dedicated'.

Her parents and two older brothers were proud of her knowledge and capabilities, but weren't entirely sold on the idea of solitary camping trips. They had tried to discourage her from traveling alone, but there was no one to make this trip with her. Her parents and brothers were busy working. Her friends all had other pursuits, or boyfriends to cultivate.

Living in New York as a child, school camps for Cassie were a constant source of information. With determination to fulfill her dream Cassie had prepared herself, learning about camping and bush craft, taking courses at college in geology and paleontology. She had even joined a rock-climbing club, but the wilderness was what she really wanted. Caving was also on her agenda, but that meant more courses at college, requiring cash. Her after-school job at the library provided that. Moving to Nevada after college was a step in the right direction.

Paleontology was in her blood, and no amount of opposition could induce her to give it up. She was, after all, over eighteen, and free to live and travel wherever she chose.

As she stood there in the hot Australian sun, wondering how she was going to get out of the mess she was in, she heard a noise behind her. Startled, she turned, shading her eyes with her hand. Surely she was hallucinating? She couldn't believe what she saw.

A dirty, rough looking man was standing next to a shady gum tree, scratching his head and staring at her. Irrelevantly, she wondered if he had six-legged passengers, or was he just sweating from the heat? She had always imagined Aussie bushmen to be wizened, bow legged with corks on their hats. This one was nothing like that; although his dusty clothes were certainly the worse for wear. He was enormous, tall and straight as the eucalyptus tree that sheltered him.

She suppressed a momentary flash of fear, telling herself not to be paranoid. This man had no intention of harming her. Travelers here were basically a live and let live, generous group of people, or so she had heard. They would help any stranded motorist in need. And she was certainly both stranded, and in need.

Cassie pulled her hair back, then picked up her wide brimmed felt hat from the ground, putting it on with a sigh of relief. As a form of protection it was minimal, but it gave her a feeling of being in charge of the situation, an illusion she was determined to make into reality.

Jack Blackwood saw before him a young woman very much like a bright flame in the sun; her hair was like fire, and it's curly abundance, before she scraped it back, had flowed over her shoulders as though alive. He wondered whether it would be hot to touch. Without thinking, Jack reached out, but moved back immediately when she scowled with distaste.

Although her face was covered in streaks of red dirt and perspiration, he could still see a freckle or two on her small nose. Jack took a step forward when he realized she was breathing erratically. He was about to ask if she was an asthmatic, when she suddenly put her hands to her mouth, taking a hasty step back.

He stopped, not wanting to frighten her. "Are you okay?" His voice curled around her nerve ends like rich dark treacle.

"Yeah, um, I'm fine." Cassie's vocal cords had dried up. She pulled off her hat, fanned her hot face with it then put it back on.

When she said nothing more, he took a tentative step, shifting his heavy pack on his shoulders to make it more comfortable.

Cassie gasped, but calmed when she saw he wasn't coming any closer. She realized that the guy in front of her wasn't going to attack, at least, not yet, and was reassured by the intelligence in his hazel eyes. He had a wide brimmed felt hat like hers, dusty brown hair hanging to his shoulders, and a scruffy beard. Standing relaxed on the road, his pack bulged with equipment. A rifle hung from his shoulder and something about him suggested he knew how to use it.

Cassie waited, silent as he quietly watched her. For the

first time in her life, she didn't know what to say. If he was dodgy, she could be in big trouble. Her brothers had taught her self-defense but, as yet, she hadn't had any opportunity to try out her skills. Nor did she really want to, especially on someone so much bigger than she. He could crush her with one swipe of his hand.

"Relax, I'm harmless." A twist at the corner of his mouth could have been a smile.

Cassie narrowed her eyes; she'd wait and see. Hoping he had a vehicle, she peered around him. Nothing. Maybe he had a camp somewhere nearby? She finally asked, "Where's your wheels? Do you think you could give me a lift?"

"No," was the stark reply. Jack was never very good with women, especially self-confident ones who know everything there is to know. He'd seen the derisive look on her face when he'd said he was harmless.

"Why not? I thought it was the rule never to leave another person stranded?" Cassie's voice took on a slightly belligerent tone. Getting an answer out of this man was like pulling teeth.

"I don't have my SUV with me," he said.

"What? I can't believe it! I actually meet someone on this road to nowhere, and he's walking!" She shook her head. "This wouldn't happen in America. I must be imagining things. No one could be that unlucky. Why are you walking? Don't you have some sort of vehicle?"

"I'm looking for botanical specimens. They're easier to find if you walk."

His scowl would normally have put her off, but Cassie was in no mood to be intimidated. She felt like drawing blood. And why couldn't the man use plain English? The word 'plants' was much more user friendly than 'botanical specimens'.

"Where are they?" she asked. "This is waste land.

Nothing green grows here. It's like Black Rock Desert in Nevada. No lakes or rivers, and I don't see any sign of rain."

Jack had no time for playing games. It was late in the day and he had his own business to attend to. He only had a few days break, taken out of a busy schedule, to follow a piece of information about an unusual plant, provided by an Aboriginal elder. "It'll rain, eventually," he said. "What's wrong with your jeep?"

"Nothing that can be fixed out here." If he could be abrupt and rude, she could too.

"How do you know that? Are you a mechanic?" He actually had the nerve to grin, his white teeth gleaming in the sun.

Cassie ground her own perfect teeth. "Look, I know what I'm talking about. The tank is damaged. All the gasoline leaked out. Okay?" She hated it when people interrogated her like that, as if she wasn't able to work things out for herself.

He was a few feet away from her and his size blocked out the sun, dwarfing Cassie's average height as they faced each other on that parched desert track. "So, what are you doing out in the middle of nowhere. If you don't mind me asking?" he asked.

"I don't mind, so long as you don't mind me telling you to mind your own business. Like the US, this is a free country. I can go anyplace I damn well please."

The man had the nerve to laugh and it made her as mad as a rattlesnake.

She took a closer look at him, not thinking much of the way he was dressed. He seemed to be a vagrant, wandering through the countryside looking for handouts. Maybe he was a sundowner? In Australia, she'd heard that was a guy who turned up to the outback station at sundown so he didn't have to do any farm work. Well, he'd struck out, she thought to herself, a trifle smugly, forgetting the plight she was in. She had nothing to give him, except a few cans of food, a mouthful of water, and a piece of advice. Don't try to intimidate a redhead. They bite.

Jack felt like reminding her he was the only human being in sight, and she needed him. He'd seen the superior expression on her face and thought, I'll teach you to be smug, lady. "Jeeps can be temperamental when they're pushed to the limit. Like women," he taunted her. He took off his pack and put it on the ground. His hat followed. "I'll take a look anyway, just to make sure." His tone said, maybe you're imagining the whole thing; you are female after all, and probably incompetent.

Cassie had a hard time keeping her mouth shut. She said, "It won't make any difference what you do to the jeep, it still won't go."

"Stubborn little thing aren't you, must be the carrot colored hair." Jack watched with interest as her lips became a thin line, and a tide of red came and went on her dirty face. She seemed to be trying to keep her mouth shut, and he wondered if she would manage it. He hoped not, there was a lot to be said for fireworks as entertainment.

He'd been hiking for days, not finding the plants he sought. A diversion would be welcome.

"My hair is not carrot, its copper," she stated. "And there's no need to get personal."

"You think I'm getting personal do you? I'm not. Sorry to disappoint. Getting personal takes time and I haven't any to spare. In case you haven't noticed, half the day's gone, so if you're sure the jeep can't be fixed, I'll be on my way. See you, girlie." He picked up his gear and hat, adjusted the straps to his broad shoulders, and proceeded in the direction of the barren hills to the north.

"Girlie?" she spluttered. "Who the hell is Girlie?" Cassie was momentarily speechless. He was leaving her, stranded in the desert. What kind of man was he?

Pausing for a moment, he looked back over his shoulder. "I suppose you know the damage can be fixed temporarily with cow dung and soap flakes. You make it into a dough with spit then shove it into the hole."

"Yuck. That's disgusting. Anyway, I don't have any soap flakes, and no cows that I can see. I'd ride one to town instead of standing here jabbering with you. There's not much use fixing the hole anyway. No gas. Can's empty."

"I suppose you're a city girl? You should have got better advice before you came out here."

Cassie hated to admit she'd miscalculated, so she kept her mouth shut. That didn't stop a low growl of frustration escaping. The hills seemed a long way away, and she realized she could be stranded for days, or weeks, if she lived that long.

Of course she had water and some food, but only for the duration of her trip; extra time spent on the road had not been allowed for. A major mistake, as it turned out.

"I don't need a critic." Cassie's tone was *not* conciliatory. "I'm perfectly familiar with the outback. I read about Australia before I came here. This is just a little glitch."

He shrugged his shoulders, as if he couldn't care less about her and her problems. "A glitch huh. I'll leave you to it then."

"Wait. You can't just leave," she called as he repositioned his pack and walked on, kicking up dust devils as he went.

"I can do anything I please. It's a free country. You told me that. Remember?" He kept walking. She hurried after him, perspiring in the heat, wishing she had a working cell phone. She'd call someone, anyone, to get her out of this mess.

"You can see I need help," she snapped, desperately afraid he would continue to walk away. Being independent was one thing. Being alone in the desert was another.

"Get a move on then. Grab your gear and follow me."

"You're not a friendly guy are you? Not like most Aussies?" she snarled. "They're willing to help. The least you could do is give me a minute to sort out my stuff."

"So, I'll wait, but not for long. Bring food and water if you've got it. That's all you'll need." He pulled back his sleeve and looked at his wristwatch.

Cassie wondered what he was doing with such a high tech instrument. He looked more suited to a Stone Age sundial. "So, what's the time on that fancy gadget?"

Jack tried not to grin. "Time we were out of here." He looked away from the girl as she hurriedly dragged things out of her jeep. He decided to move on slowly, but was quite a way along the dusty red track before she'd got her things together.

She picked up her sleeping bag and pack, following him, scowling as if he were the cause of all her problems. A long-suffering martyr she was not. He felt every one of the darts she mentally flung at his back.

He hoped she had the sense to bring only necessary stuff. In his experience, women were hopeless at packing, weighing themselves down with a lot of unnecessary clutter.

His sister, Ronnie, was a perfect example of disorganized packing. He avoided getting caught up in it, knowing he would never be right, no matter what he said.

"Wait for me," she called. When he didn't stop, she yelled, "Can't you wait a bit? This stuff is heavy."

"Leave some of it behind," he advised, and kept on walking.

"I need everything I've got, Jack," she snapped.

"How did you know my name?" He stopped and turned, immediately suspicious.

"I didn't. Every guy in the Australian outback is 'Jack'. Everyone knows that."

"Right." Jack wanted to kick himself for reacting to her use of his name. 'Jack' could be anyone, or no one. He would remember if he had met her before. She was unforgettable. She made his palms tingle and sweat just looking at her.

"What's your name?" he asked, before he could stop himself. He didn't really want to know anything about her. She was just a stranger, passing through. Asking what she was doing alone out in the desert would be asking for the story of her life. He had too much going on to get involved, even if he wanted to.

"Cassie."

"Well, Cassie, quit complaining and get a move on. I want to be at my camp before next week," he said, walking on, not seeming to allow for her inability to keep up.

Cassie fumed. He was impossible. "What do you mean, next week?" Cassie's words were like bullets.

"It's a fair hike to where I'm camped, about two or three days walk I reckon."

"What! You have to be kidding. I can't walk that far." She stopped walking. Her unwilling companion simply kept on going, without saying another word.

"Hey, come back here!" Cassie was furious. Ignorant oaf, she thought, I'll teach you to ignore me. "You could at least pretend to be a gentleman and help me with my things. They're heavy."

"Who said I was a gentleman?" Jack stopped, looking back at her. He tried to hide his expression, sensing a grin would be the last straw. The theory about red hair being a clue to a person's temperament was certainly true in this case. If looks could kill, he thought, I'd be lying in the road waiting for crows to peck my eyes out.

Cassie awkwardly redistributed her load on her shoulders and walked on, thinking of all the things she would like to do to him, as soon as she didn't need him any more.

Most of those thoughts were tinged with retribution, but others crept in as she observed his long lean stride and his broad strong back. What she would like to do to him mutated into what she would like to do with him. She tried to stop her hands tingling as she imagined what it would be like to touch that warm hard flesh, to make him look at her with admiration, rather than disdain.

She scowled ferociously, rejecting those heat-making thoughts for the more immediate satisfaction of Jack tied up on an ant's nest baking slowly in the sun as he squirmed. Now that was satisfying, and possibly a little more achievable.

Jack knew what she was thinking. The expression on her face, when he looked back every now and then to check that she hadn't fallen in the roadway, was a dead giveaway. It gave him no end of amusement. The imaginary darts in his back should have killed him, or at least laid him out for a few hours.

He refused to think about the other expression he'd caught hovering on her face when she thought he wasn't looking. The need in her eyes as they roved over his body struck him with the force of a sledgehammer, far too dangerous for his peace of mind.

He wanted to say, 'I feel it too', but didn't dare. If he said, and did, what he wanted to do, they might never get out of the desert alive. They'd be too damn tired to walk anywhere.

After about an hour Cassie called out to the drill sergeant in front of her. "Hey you, Jack, can we stop for a drink now?" It was not a request.

Jack stopped, turning around to look at her. "Okay, but don't drink more than half a cup at a time. What we've got has to last until we reach camp tomorrow afternoon."

"I haven't got more than a quart… err, two liters with me. I thought there'd be water somewhere around." Cassie's voice was tinged with weariness. "There's a creek on the map."

He raised his eyes up to the heavens, saying, "Give me strength." Then he looked at Cassie. "You haven't got a clue have you? You're like a child, unprepared to live in a hostile world. How could you come out here, camping alone, without knowing the first thing about survival? It was suicide."

He was angry at her blind ignorance. She could die out here and no one would know until her dried bones were found, possibly years later. Maybe they'd never be found?

Irritated by his abrasive tone, she replied with heat. "I'm not a child. I've spent a lot of time on my own, camping out. I've survived just fine up until now, thank you very much." She glared at him and thought; you think you know everything, Jack.

"Up to now you've survived. But it's more by blind luck or God's grace than good management. You're out of your league, little girl, and one day, if you keep ignoring basic rules, you won't survive. Your family would never even find your body out here, the dingoes would beat them to it." He looked at her with piercing eyes. "Dingoes are meat eaters in case you were wondering. Like wolves."

"That's not what I wanted to hear." She glared at him, her face red, covered with sweat and dirt. She had never felt so dishevelled in her life. Trouble was, she felt as wild as she looked. Was it true about dingoes? Would they really eat her? "I've seen dingoes in the zoo. I'm sure they're quite harmless to people. They don't look savage to me."

"Perhaps we can find a wild pack of them. You can find out first hand?"

"No. I don't think so." She knew right then she'd probably fit right in with the pack. Acting like a savage was getting to be a habit. "Can we get going now?"

"Yes. But go easy on the water. I haven't any spare if you drink yours too quickly."

Cassie was too exhausted to argue so she forced herself to continue to walk in his large dusty footprints, unable at the moment, to appreciate the beauty of terracotta sand or wide blue skies. "Walk slower can't you?" She hated the pleading note in her voice, hated him, needing him too, for survival. "The stones are rough on my boots."

"No. Going slow is out. We need to get as far as possible before it gets dark."

Cassie stopped walking. "Afraid of the dark, are you? What a joke. I thought you weren't afraid of anything."

"If I was, I'd never tell you. You'd eat me alive. The night brings out all kinds of predators." At her look, he said, "Not me. I'm a peaceful guy, most of the time. You'd better get moving or I'll leave you behind. You'd make a tasty side dish for a wild boar, or," he grinned suddenly, "a hungry possum."

"They're vegetarians," she stated positively. "I worked in a library in New York so I read a lot of books before I came to Australia."

He laughed. "You should have read about desert survival skills. That could have saved your life, if I hadn't come along."

"So, I got lucky."

"Yeah. You did. Look up there." He pointed up. "Crows need to eat too."

Cassie saw black specs flying high in the sky and shuddered, her imagination working overtime. Jack grinned. "Don't worry. They're eagles, not crows."

"Really? I would love it if they'd land. Seeing eagles up close would be incredible."

"They're smart. Man is the predator around here, so they stay out of reach."

"Aren't they protected?"

"Yeah. Doesn't seem to make much difference to some people. There are huge fines for killing protected species, but it still goes on. I've seen Australian birds, rare parrots mostly, packed in boxes at the airports, on the way to foreign countries. Half of them are dead by the time they get there."

Cassie scowled. "I hate that. I'd like to give those hunters a taste of their own medicine."

"What, pack them in boxes and send them overseas?"

"Yeah. That's it. They'd be packed in really tight."

"Like sardines," agreed Jack.

Cassie wondered how someone like Jack could end up a bum, wandering in the desert. He seemed intelligent and resourceful, but there was some sort of mystery about him. She longed to discover the answer, even though she sensed it could be dangerous to her peace of mind. The more she discovered, the more she would want to know.

Silence prevailed as they trudged on through the afternoon. Red dust rose in the wake of their footprints; two very large followed by two small. It was hours later when Jack called a halt. Cassie sat down at the edge of the road, recovering. It was almost evening and the air was cooling down. She was accustomed to the heat, but hiking in it was hard. Jack was a slave driver. Cassie vowed there and then never to be his slave.

Jack wondered what had brought Cassie out to this part of Australia. There was nothing much in this area of the Northern Territory for tourists, and yet, here she was, traveling alone in the desert like an amateur hiker on a suburban nature trail. Darwin and Alice Springs were much more tourist friendly. At least they had water.

"What are you doing out here?" he asked bluntly. "This is hard country." He grinned suddenly, bringing an unexpected gleam to his hazel eyes, "Even for someone as survival conscious as you claim to be."

"I'm looking for dinosaur bones," she replied. "Paleontology is an interest of mine."

"If you're not careful, the only bones to be found will be your own." Jack frowned, as a vision of her lying lifeless in the desert came to him. He barely controlled a shudder.

Cassie's eyes flashed. "Why don't you stop telling me what to do? I didn't ask you to comment on my life. For that matter, what about you? You're taking a chance out here. Walking to find plants, oh, I'm sorry, botanical specimens must be just as dangerous. What about snakes? You're flesh and blood, like me. I'm just as able to survive out here as you are. Perhaps more able because I, at least, have a means of transport."

"You did." He gave a cracked laugh. "But now we're even. We both have to walk."

Cassie wanted to hit him because, damn it, he was right.

"Let's get on with it then," she snapped. "We don't want to be late getting to camp, do we? It might upset your plans."

"We'll have to spend the night on the road anyway." He was extremely satisfied with the expression that crossed her dusty face. It spoke volumes about the way she felt; she was angry, frustrated, exhausted. He knew he could relieve her anxieties but decided to let her stew for a while. Some lessons needed to be learned the hard way.

She shouldn't look down on someone less fortunate than herself, he thought. She had wheels and he didn't! How ironic was that? What use was a vehicle without fuel? He chuckled to himself as they set off once more along the road. This was going to be fun, but he would probably be the only one laughing.

A while later Cassie stopped. "Ouch! She hopped along on one foot, trying to rid herself of something in her boot. "Slow down a minute will you?" she called. "I've got to off-load some gravel." She sat down at the side of the road

Jack strolled back, thinking she was looking very worn around the edges. He decided to give her a break. She'd earned it. She hadn't complained, or said a word, for at least an hour. Or maybe it was just that her throat was clogged with fine red sand? Like his?

"Okay, we'll rest here." He went to the other side of the track, sitting on a bare piece of earth, leaning back on his pack with a barely acknowledged sigh of relief. It had been hard going, and his admiration for his companion was growing. She'd done well, but wouldn't she gloat if he said so? He'd never hear the end of it.

Suddenly Cassie started to shriek, slapping her legs,

writhing on the ground. Jack jumped up, rushing to her side. He realized something was seriously wrong, and then he saw what was happening. A large nest of meat ants was stirring under her.

They had discovered that a tasty dish had landed on their territory, and they wanted it. He could almost hear them smacking their lips, if ants had lips? Maybe they just had pincers? Sharp, serrated pincers. Jack had to move, fast. The idea of Cassie's tender flesh being bitten was unthinkable.

Ants were rushing about in a frenzy, attempting to eat, but finding it very tough going. Denim wasn't on their selected menu, plus their unexpected banquet was trying to escape. They renewed their efforts to chew, sending their snack into a state of hysteria as they found their way past tough jeans and lacy pink underwear. Some even found their way past socks and leather boots.

Jack hurriedly began slapping the ants swarming over Cassie's legs and bottom while physically dragging her away from the nest. She was oblivious to all modesty as he rapidly dragged her boots and socks off, undoing the zip on her jeans, stripping them from her body. He threw them away, and then brushed the remaining ants off her legs, revealing quite a number of bites. She was unable to stop sobbing, her breathing harsh.

Trembling from head to foot, Cassie leaned weakly on Jack's chest, finding it enormously soothing. She wondered what a shaggy, uncouth vagrant could offer in the way of comfort and, to her surprise, found the answer in solid muscle encasing a frame built to withstand almost anything. His soft murmur of reassurance flowed through her, turning her bones to jelly. As a port in a storm, he was perfect.

"Are you okay?" he asked, stroking her long hair back

from her face, the trembling of his hand barely noticeable, now that the urgency was past. The ant attack had brought him out in a cold sweat, not the kind of chill he would have chosen for himself.

"I think so. Thanks. I was really scared." Cassie looked up at him with eyes that were filled with gratitude. It was replaced immediately with other concerns. She couldn't stop scratching. "Damn bites. They itch and sting at the same time. Did they bite you too?"

"Not much. Don't worry. I've got some antiseptic cream in my pack." His confident voice calmed her as he drew her further away from the nest, but still she scratched. Suddenly she realized that she was standing in the road, half naked, with a man she had only just met, an unknown quantity. What was she doing, allowing him to see her like this, vulnerable and afraid? What would her family say? Probably 'serve you right for going alone to Australia in the first place'.

She would have died from embarrassment, but Jack brought out the antiseptic cream, and all she could feel then was appreciation at his thoughtfulness. He had to be a prince in disguise, or at the very least a gentleman. He looked so concerned, and didn't make any of the smart remarks her brothers would in the same situation. Yes, he was definitely a prince. It was a shame she didn't look like a princess. She'd have to take a bath for that to happen, but there wasn't any water, or soap. Not even a towel.

"This should help," he said. Carefully, he applied balm to her legs and, to her embarrassment, the other portions of her bitten anatomy, disposing of ant corpses along the way.

She found herself thinking he should have been a doctor; he had such a soothing touch. The way he treated her had improved significantly when she needed immediate assistance. He had been there for her, and that was what mattered.

When he had finished anointing all the bites he could find, she rushed to get her jeans, hurriedly shaking them before pulling them on and buttoning up her shirt. Jack looked on with amusement, plus a measure of male appreciation. The ants had stirred her up, and she'd done the same for him. "No more places for me to put ointment on?" he inquired hopefully, his tone less of the gentleman now, and more of the male.

"Thank you. I'm okay now. We'd better get moving." Cassie's blush, hidden under her sun burnt cheeks, betrayed itself when she refused to look Jack in the eye. She didn't want to read what was on his mind, having enough trouble with her own vivid imagination. "It's getting late and you wanted to reach camp in a hurry, didn't you?"

"Yeah, I'm in a hurry," he agreed, wondering what had happened. He'd felt strangely protective when she was in his arms, needing him. Perhaps he'd been too long without a woman? That thought bothered him. Damned female, reminding him that he was human, and male. All he had to do was go into town for some action if that was where his hormones were leading him. He wished they would give it a rest, for now.

When the sun slipped behind the hills, streams of crimson and gold spread themselves across the sky. The air cooled, and the birds came out for a final look around as Jack and Cassie made camp in a small grove of trees. They put their packs up into tree branches to prevent anything crawling in during the night.

Jack inspected the ground for ant nests while Cassie gathered firewood, finding a convenient tree at the same time. Bathrooms were nonexistent so she had to make do.

She was unable to relax. Although he seemed trustworthy, she reminded herself that she didn't really know this man. She had always trusted her ability to assess a situation, but with this stranger, sitting close enough to touch, suddenly she felt vulnerable, as if she couldn't see clearly any more.

Uncomfortable with her thoughts, Cassie decided to go with her instincts and find out a little more about her companion. She'd know if he was inventing stories, having heard enough fiction from her brothers. After he had emptied a packet of dried soup into a saucepan of water and put it onto the flames, she began to ask questions.

"Tell me about yourself, Jack. What are you really doing out here?"

"I'm just a guy on the move, looking for plants. That's all."

"Well then, Jack, don't you want to know what I'm doing here?"

He shrugged. "What is there to know? You're from the US. You can't fix jeeps and your survival skills are limited. And you don't like ants. Is that how it goes?

"You did save my life back there. That makes us connected, somehow."

"I suppose you'll tell me about yourself, whether I want to know or not?" This was precisely why he didn't go out much with women. They always wanted to talk, and they wanted a man to talk back. It was hard, especially when he had nothing to say.

"You don't have to be like that, Jack. I'm just trying to be civilized. The least you can do is be civilized back."

Jack thought, with an internal snarl, I don't want to be civilized. I want to take this woman and give her what she's asking for, right there on the hard, desert track. Denial was hard, too, but he did it. His voice almost normal, he asked, "So, your name is Cassie. Cassie What?"

"Travis. I'm Cassiopeia Travis. I'll spell it for you, if you like." She spelled it slowly and carefully.

"Don't worry. I get it. What sort of weird name is that?" he asked in a tone of disbelief. He was a man of science, not a classical scholar. He'd heard of Cassiopeia, but didn't know anyone who used the name, until now. It seemed to suit her.

"My mother loves to read Greek mythology. I was named after her favorite character. Cassiopeia was Andromeda's mother. She bragged about her daughter being more beautiful than Poseidon's sea nymphs. Big mistake. Poseidon wanted Andromeda fed to his sea monster so she wound up chained to a rock."

"I've heard of Andromeda. That's a galaxy isn't it?"

"It is now. Back then it was a girl, flesh and blood like me."

Jack swallowed hard. He knew Cassie was flesh and blood. He'd held her in his arms and felt every one of her soft curves. He never thought he'd be grateful to ants, but he was. "So what happened? Did the sea monster get his dinner?"

Cassie frowned. "It's not funny, Jack. Andromeda was being sacrificed."

"Sorry." Jack tried to look chastened. "Did Andromeda get eaten, after all that?"

"No. Perseus rescued her. He was the son of Zeus so he had a lot going for him. She married him so it all worked out in the end. Even Cassiopeia was happy."

"So can I call you Cassiopeia? Classy name."

"You can call me Cassie. It's much easier for someone of limited intelligence." She looked for a reaction from him. It came immediately.

"You've got a smart mouth," he accused as he stirred the pot on the fire. Jack's bush craft skills were honed to perfection, but his social graces needed quite a deal of polish before they were up to acceptable standard. Cassie decided to educate him.

She opened her mouth to speak, but he cut in. "Listen, if I'm cooking you're collecting firewood, so cut the small talk and get on with it, Cassiopeia. Otherwise I'll find something else for you to do."

His grin had turned wickedly suggestive as he scanned his versatile imagination for something to occupy her time. It didn't take long since he'd already been down that road.

Reading his mind fairly accurately, and trying to downplay the tide of red on her face, Cassie said under her breath, "Dictator."

"I heard that." Then he grinned and said, "You'll keep."

She said, "Hah. So will you," and laughed as she disappeared into the trees.

She was a breath of fresh air to a man who was dedicated to his profession, and too serious in his pursuit of perfection. He was rarely satisfied; nothing ever seemed good enough to suit him. He knew this was a flaw in his nature and acknowledged that he needed to break out now and then, have some fun. It seemed as if fun had come to him in the irresistible shape of Cassie, red headed torment, possibly Greek, possibly a Goddess, time would tell. He only hoped the situation wouldn't get too far out of his control. She would be like a firestorm in his blood, once unleashed she would be unstoppable.

Two

THE campfire shot sparks that night as Jack and Cassie shared a mug of tea after a packet meal of chicken soup heated with water. Cassie watched him, still wary as she ate, not really wanting much food, but not knowing how to occupy her time. Any conversation had dried up at Jack's monosyllabic replies. She decided to try again.

"What's the rifle for?" she asked.

"Rabbits." When she opened her mouth to ask another question he said, "Protein."

"Oh. I thought you might be looking for wild pigs." Cassie yawned.

"Not especially." Jack looked away and said, "Go to sleep. I'll keep watch."

"Thanks. But who'll watch you?"

"I'll watch me as well. Don't worry; I'm not planning to attack you. I've been out here for months. I haven't assaulted anybody yet."

"Well, if you think I'm a good way to break the drought, think again. I've got two brothers who taught me how to take care of myself."

"Good. Now that's over and desire for your ant bitten body has been quelled, you can sleep. I won't come knocking on your door." Telling stories was getting to be a habit, one he didn't want to break, not yet.

"Good. I don't have a door, and you weren't invited anyway."

Cassie couldn't stay awake. When she crawled into her sleeping bag, she fell asleep immediately. Jack made his own bed on the other side of the fire, watching her for a while, his expression thoughtful in the flickering firelight. Why would an American girl travel alone in the Australian outback? It was a dangerous place for the inexperienced.

She moved in her sleep, lifting a slender naked arm out of the covers. He moved over to her and put out his hand, intending to cover her up.

When he touched the warm flesh of her arm, Jack's senses took over, and instead of helping her, he found himself wanting to help himself, to touch her again, and go on touching her until she was as hot as he was.

He watched Cassie hungrily as he listened to her breathing, the gentle movement of her breasts sending signals to his senses, and other parts of his anatomy. He was the hunter and she was his prey. Any resemblance to civilized man was purely coincidental.

As he hovered between primal instincts and empathy for the innocent girl lying before him, sparks from the fire shot into the air, dispelling the feeling of unreality that had come over him. This was dreamtime country, but he was definitely dreaming if he thought he could take what he wanted without repercussions. Quickly, before he claimed the prize he wanted, he retreated to the other side of the fire.

Jack realized that he had no choice but to take care of this girl, but couldn't understand why he was enjoying his run-ins with her also. She should have been a thorn in his flesh; instead she was a rose, tempting him beyond endurance.

He had always been a solitary man, content to work and study, occasionally taking a girl out for dinner, never having any desire for anything more permanent. There had been one exception. A girl a few years older than himself, an exchange student from America, had come to stay with his family when he was seventeen. That was quite an experience for a naive young man, he had never forgotten how it had felt to be absorbed by another person, to be given the freedom to explore, and be explored. He had fallen in love with her in minutes; it had taken years to accept and forgive her for moving on.

Any involvement with women had been kept strictly under control after that, he had made sure. Now, at thirty-one, he thought he would be immune to temptation.

Of course he had natural male urges, satisfying them when he could, but he usually preferred the company of women who were more interested in their careers than social events, women who could have a lively conversation, not leaving him bored out of his mind. At least Cassie wasn't boring. Instead he found her riveting, and fun.

Fun was not a priority in his life, although he could remember times when he had enjoyed family get-togethers. His mother was a busy woman, his father an engineer. Theirs was a quiet home, he and his sister, Ronnie, grew up in an academic atmosphere, the emphasis on achievement.

Remembering how his parents had rarely raised their voices, keeping noise to a minimum, Jack realized his life had mirrored their attitudes without his true nature surfacing. Since he had encountered Cassie however, he had been shaken out of his rut and hurled into orbit. She was lively and interesting, and he decided he'd been missing an important ingredient in his life. It was time to change his habits and cultivate a little more excitement. He grinned with anticipation. Perhaps he wasn't so staid after all? Certainly, after watching over her by the fire, he realized his primitive reaction to her was completely out of line, but it felt incredible to feel that burst of adrenalin. It was like being let out of jail after many years of solitary confinement.

Jack was deeply asleep when someone shouting woke him. Cassie, wriggling around in her sleeping bag, was still asleep. She was yelling, "Get off me," and waving her arms.

He realized that she was dreaming about ants and decided to wake her. It was almost dawn and it was better to get moving early before the sun rose on another hot day.

The trees around them were host to many insects and small creatures, the largest of which were possums. Hardly visible, the small creatures watched them with small black eyes, alert for danger. Jack had an apple left over in his pack, so he cut it up and left it on the ground for a possum breakfast.

He crouched down to Cassie, crooning close to her ear. "Cassie, Sweetheart, wake up." He touched her shoulder, feeling her velvety skin respond with heat. Her soft copper hair curled over his hand, pulling him closer. It seemed like she moved towards him, but he couldn't be sure.

You don't want to get involved with her, Jack reminded himself. It was too bad his hands seemed to have a mind of their own. They stayed, stroking her skin as if it were essential to his survival. Women are more trouble than they're worth, he advised his overloaded hormones, but deep down, he knew he was kidding himself; of course he wanted to get involved, deeply involved. She awoke feelings in him of an intensity he had never known, even with his first girlfriend.

His strong desire to protect Cassie made the situation a catch 22. Damned if he did, damned if he didn't. How could he make love to her? He was a man with trouble in his life, a man with a stressful job, commitments, so how could he make promises he could not keep? That would be no protection at all.

Cassie turned over restlessly. Jack jerked backwards, overbalancing, falling on his rear end. Ruefully he picked himself up, calling her again, this time from a short distance away. "Cassie, wake up. Time to go."

If she managed to accidentally floor him when she was asleep, what havoc could she cause when fully awake, and intending to do him a mischief? An anticipatory gleam lit his smoky hazel eyes.

He contemplated returning to her side, offering to keep her ant-ridden nightmares away. Too bad his conscience was such a hard taskmaster. Anyway, he was sure she would see through his ruse in no time.

He reflected that people always wanted what they should not, or could not, have, and, much to his disgust, he was no exception. Self-control was won at a price.

Cassie came reluctantly awake, sitting up in her makeshift bed, yawning and rubbing her eyes, still scratching her bitten arms and legs. "It's still dark. What's going on, Jack? I hope there aren't any more ants. I think I'm allergic."

"No ants. Not here. We're just making an early start." Jack handed her the tube of antiseptic cream before turning towards the pile of twigs and small branches that she had gathered the night before. He set about lighting a fire. "You go off and do what's necessary. I'll make breakfast."

"Thanks," she said hesitantly. "Just a drink will do. I don't eat breakfast. I don't suppose you have coffee?"

"No coffee. Sorry."

She nodded her understanding, then made her way past a few trees to find a clump of bushes. It was primitive, but she managed to attend to her needs, giving herself a wash with a cupful of precious water. She returned to camp feeling refreshed.

Jack had a pot of tea ready. Cassie drank it as if it were nectar, grateful for the drink but not the early morning call. "Do you always get up halfway through the night? It's still too dark to see anything." She yawned and rubbed her eyes, lifting arms above her head to stretch.

"It's not too dark to walk," he said gruffly, trying not to look at her, not to think about what he was missing out on. "The sun is coming up so let's get moving."

They hurriedly packed, starting out just as the sky became awash with the glorious colors of sunrise, brilliant crimson over all with lesser shades of orange, amber and, finally blue.

Cassie turned to Jack. "It's beautiful out here, such a vast endless sky. You can see the stars clearly. So different from the city. Back there everything seems to smell and taste of pollution. I think it's the exhaust fumes at morning peak hour that do it. The daylight is different here too, brighter somehow. I never get tired of it."

The eager light faded from her face when he replied with apparent indifference. "It's great, but don't waste time. There's going to be a storm."

"What, in this clear sky? Surely you're imagining things?"

"No, I'm not. You know the saying, red sky at night, shepherd's delight. Well don't forget, red sky in the morning, shepherd's warning."

"That's just an old wives tale," she scoffed.

"It seems to work well enough around here," he said.

"Old wives knew a lot of useful stuff. Come on. We can reach Kalangadoo by early afternoon if we don't stop for lunch."

"What's Kalangadoo?" asked Cassie.

"That's where my camp is. It's a lake on a tributary of the Plenty River. There's spring water to drink and we'll be able to fish. There's nothing like fresh fish for dinner."

"How did you know about it?"

"It's just a place I found while I was plant hunting. It's not on any map I've ever seen. An old Aboriginal stockman told me its name, and I always go there when I pass through this area on the way to Jasper Creek." He heaved his pack more comfortably on his broad shoulders. "It's a good spot to take a break."

Jack strode along with Cassie trailing behind like a camp follower. How archaic she thought, unable to think of herself as a follower of any kind. Women should be self-reliant, her mother had told her, and she had to agree.

She wasn't about to follow Jack's orders without question, no matter if she found him distracting, with his warm caressing hands and eyes that seemed to see into her soul.

He was quite ruthless, she thought, forcing her to keep walking even when she was obviously exhausted. She watched him stride ahead of her, long legs eating away the miles as though they were nothing, his strong back carrying the jumbo-sized pack with ease. She tried to imagine him without his long hair and beard, and failed. He seemed to be an inconsistency within himself, an unkempt, roughly dressed traveler with perfect teeth and a beautiful deep voice, speaking English without swearing crudely or using unintelligible slang. Something didn't match up. Even his fingernails were clean.

Underneath all that hair, there lurked a smile that was guaranteed to cause havoc in even the hardest female heart. What a contradiction, thought Cassie, like two sides of a coin, one side rough, one side smooth. She wasn't sure which side she liked best.

While the wind and sun burned Cassie's face, creating more freckles across her small nose, the shade of a large gum tree beckoned enticingly. Sunlight blinded her as she made her way through grass and small trees to sit beneath its branches. "Have you checked for ants?" Jack asked, with a straight face. "They'll be watching out for you."

She jumped up like a startled rabbit. "Oh no, not those little beasts again," and only relaxed when she saw the area was clear of miniature livestock. She realized then that he had been teasing and grinned. "One of these days I'm going to get you."

"I'm counting on it," he said enigmatically.

Jack leaned against the tree, watching her for a moment, and then he asked, "What's with this fossil hunting thing anyway? Is it your job or what?"

"Not exactly."

"Well, do you get paid for looking, or do you hope to get paid when you find something?"

"Well, a bit of both I suppose. I could get another job in a library, but this is what I love to do. Waitress work puts food on the table but I'd give it up in a minute if I thought paleontology would pay enough. As it is, I write articles about the subject for the occasional magazine. I'm not a journalist though. After I came to Australia from Nevada, I camped near Lake Callabonna in South Australia."

"That's quite a way from here. What were you doing there?" His questions seemed mildly curious and non-threatening, so she relaxed her usual guard and answered him in the same vein.

"I was looking around. A few years ago some giant diprotodon bones were discovered there. I was looking around the area for about two weeks, searching for any other fossils or bones, but that dig is just about worked out so I came up this way. I was trying to get up north to Alcoota. There have been some important finds there."

"What's a dipro-whatever? Is that some kind of dinosaur?"

"Not quite. A diprotodon is the largest marsupial that ever lived. They were herbivores and looked a bit like a rhinoceros only much bigger. Some people say they looked like a big wombat."

"Interesting." Jack drew his brows together; "I've seen shells and fish fossils around here. They'd be relics of the inland sea that once covered this area wouldn't they?"

"Yes, I've seen plenty myself, but I'm after something more controversial. Lucy Creek is another place that sounded promising. It's off the Plenty Highway, towards Mt. Isa. I might try my luck around that area next. I believe some larger fossil bones have been found in an exposed dry creek bed. I read something about a giant lizard, a giant goanna."

"Not something you'd miss if you were driving. You're out of luck as far as moving on to Alcoota goes. It's too far to walk. Without transport, you'll have to make do with Kalangadoo."

"You can get someone to help can't you? Isn't there a cattle station around here? They have trucks, and airplanes. I could get a ride."

"Yes, but the cattle station would take days to walk to. Does your family know where you are?"

"Not really. Oh, they know I'm in Australia, in the Northern Territory, but that's all." Cassie suddenly realized she shouldn't have said that. It was foolish to confess such things to a man she didn't really know, even though he seemed harmless enough. Who knew what kind of tricks the guy had up his sleeve?

Thinking of sleeves, Cassie looked at Jack's, immediately aware of hard muscles and strength. She looked up, her eyes coming in contact with warm, hazel eyes, laden with an instinctive knowledge of her needs. She blinked. She was sure she was imagining things. He couldn't want her like that, surely. There had been no indication...

Cassie was brought back abruptly from fantasy-land when Jack asked, "So, unless your family report you missing, no-one will give a damn what you get up to?" He sighed. "Did you file your travel plans with the police by any chance?"

"Sure I did." Cassie's face flushed with guilt, as her tormentor looked at her with searching eyes. "Oh, all right. I would have but I didn't know it was illegal not to say where I was headed. It wasn't a priority. The dinosaur bones were waiting and I was in a hurry. So arrest me. I'll come quietly."

"It's not illegal, Cassie. Thinking ahead in case of problems was a better plan."

While Cassie fumed at his derision, Jack was thinking, what was that about coming quietly? Who wants quiet?

All Jack wanted was Cassie, any way he could get her. All he needed was patience.

"What's done is done, Jack," she huffed.

"You can forget about being picked up by a stray motorist out here. Out on this track they don't exist."

"What do you mean?"

"Look around you. See any cars?"

"Obviously not," she snapped. "So why not call for

help? Surely a clever guy like you has a cell phone? You seem to have everything else in that pack."

"Very funny. I would have used it by now if I had one that worked. I left it behind at my base camp."

"Hey, mine's dead too. I thought it was broken so I left it with my jeep."

"A cell phone wouldn't work out here anyway. We're miles away from civilization and besides, rocky hills block signals. So, as you can see, we're on our own out here. Just you and me and the wildlife."

"Are you saying we've walked all this way in the dust and heat for nothing? I thought you would have had a working cell phone at your camp. I was counting on it."

"Would you rather I left you in the road to die of hunger and thirst?" Jack knew his words would infuriate her, loving it when she came back at him with a peppery answer, her eyes spitting fire.

"Someone else would have come along eventually. I would have been rescued."

"No, you wouldn't. You would have become dehydrated and delirious." He was deliberately brutal to impress upon her the danger of ignoring safety precautions in the outback.

"You know, I think my first impression of you was right." Cassie was developing a full head of steam.

"I won't ask what it was. I can guess."

"I'll tell you anyway. I thought you were some sort of crazy hermit who was walking around out here because he wasn't able to get along with other people."

"You want to be careful then, girlie." He leered at her. "I might really be crazy and then you'd be in trouble. There's only you and me, and a couple hundred ants out here. I could do whatever I pleased. No-one would ever find out." His grin was evil, a taunt. "Do you understand what I'm saying?"

Cassie wasn't about to let his intimidating size get to her. She told herself she could handle anyone, even him. She steeled herself not to show his words had worried her. "Trying to scare me are you, Jack? It won't happen. I can take care of myself. I told you, my brothers have been teaching me karate since I was big enough to bite their kneecaps." She didn't add that she had never won a tussle, not once.

Jack had a momentary vision of two grown men being wrestled to the ground by Cassie. Trying not to show his amusement, he bit down on his lower lip. If he laughed out loud, the rest of the trip would be as silent as the grave. She might never forgive him. He didn't know if he could live with that.

In the late afternoon of the second day they reached a water hole. Mosquitoes were raising weals on Cassie's arms; she was again scratching herself raw.

Her feet were burning with blisters. She was bone weary, but Jack still looked as fit as he had that morning. It was a situation that really got under her skin.

"That water looks wonderful." She sighed. "I've got bites on my bites and blisters on my blisters. My feet could do with a good soak."

"Yeah. Mine too. This is Kalangadoo." Narrowing his keen eyes, Jack looked over the water. "My camp's already set up on the side of that hill over there."

Turning to watch Cassie slap mosquitoes, he hoped he was doing the right thing, bringing her with him. It was safe for the moment, but who could tell what the future would hold. This was a dangerous place for inexperienced travelers. Responsibility for her safety was gnawing at him, but as he watched her, and saw the fire in her soul for adventure, he wanted to be a part of it. He'd even check out prehistoric bones if it made her happy. Looking for rare plants was an interesting and consuming occupation, but sometimes he wanted to break out and enjoy life. All he had to do was remember how.

Something besides the girl's safety was knotting his stomach. It could be hunger, but it was probably something much more primal.

Not wanting to go there, he said, "It's not too far now, a quick hike through those trees."

"Give me a break," Cassie moaned tiredly, closing her eyes against the glare. "I'm not sure I'm ready for a quick anything." Once again she cursed her unruly mouth. It had gotten her into more trouble than it was worth.

"I'm not into quickies myself," Jack said slowly, his expression deadpan. "I like to take my time and do the job thoroughly."

She looked at him with suspicion. Was that Jack teasing? No, couldn't be. He was a serious guy, not a joker. She groaned. "I'm not going to get into that one. I haven't the energy. Come on. Let's go find your camp before I fall in a heap."

Cassie's spirits lifted when she saw the flocks of birds. Low hills surrounding the water were covered with native bushes, interspersed by a few larger gum trees. It was a place where sparse vegetation and mud edged the water while smaller trees provided shade. In some areas where the shade was thin, mud had dried in the hot sun and cracked. Further out, red dust gathered up in spirals and whirled away with the wind. Up a gum tree, a goanna basked in the sun; the only sign of life a slowly swishing tail.

Cassie longed for a wash, but she knew it could be dangerous to swim in or drink unknown waters. Animals had been known to die during droughts leaving carcasses rotting, poisoning the water. She looked around and saw that it was unlikely to be poisoned, fresh prints scattered around showed that many animals had been drinking here.

Jack said, "Water doesn't look toxic. You can swim." He smiled, looking around eagerly as he strode along, following the river as it widened to form the water hole, then flowed on towards the south.

Cassie realized that she would have to be resourceful if she were going to get back to civilization. There was no one she could ask for help; her guide had made it obvious that he wasn't going to put himself out on her account. In his search for rare plants, he was more interested in the scenery than her. She reminded herself to be grateful. He wasn't Jack the ripper, just Jack the plant guy. It could have been much worse.

As they walked Cassie scanned the vast expanse of sky, noticing a change in the weather. She could smell the moisture in the air and see dark thunderclouds on the horizon, forewarning a possible storm. Research of Australia's weather patterns gave her some understanding of the monsoon season, when waterways across Australia's north filled and flooded their banks with life-giving rain.

"How much further, Jack?" Cassie asked. "I'm beat. Maybe a swim would help?"

She longed for a wash and the water looked perfect, cool and inviting. There was no sign of wildlife, either dead on the riverbank, or alive. Birds were a different story. They were everywhere, both on the wing, and ducking for food in the water, their long beaks brimming with fish.

"You can see my camp from here." He pointed to a

small flat area on the side of a hill well above the water's edge. Trees and scrub almost hid it from view. "You can swim when we get there."

"Is there supposed to be a tent there?" she asked.

"There is one. You can't see it because of the bark that covers it."

"What's that in aid of?"

"Insulation and camouflage. It's very effective. Nothing can be seen from the air."

His words made her look curiously at him. Was he hiding from someone? She decided to be on the alert just in case. "Is there any reason you don't want to be seen from the air? I'd like it if a plane came over. I could signal and get a lift back to civilization."

Jack grinned. "It's because of birds. I photograph them. If they see human occupation in a place, they don't land. It's as simple as that." Somehow the answer came a bit too easily. Instead of lessening her suspicions, his story highlighted her lack of knowledge about him. She decided not to question him further in case he became alert to her frame of mind. He was still an unknown quantity and that edge of danger seemed to be always hovering over him, and by proximity, over her.

Still the inoffensive bushman, Jack said, "We have to do a bit of climbing so we won't be eaten in our beds." He chuckled at the way she received this revelation.

"I won't be able to sleep with that threat hanging over my head. Just what is going to eat us? Ants?" She shuddered as she remembered her encounter with them.

Jack replied seriously, "Savage creatures that enjoy tender flesh like yours. Just check your boots for scorpions and other livestock before you put them on."

"Is that all I have to worry about? What about

poisonous snakes, or dangerous animals, like echidnas or wombats? How about crocodiles?"

"Echidnas, being anteaters, only eat ants. You should approve of that, Cassie. Revenge is sweet. Wombats are inoffensive but tiger snakes are another story. They'll come after you at certain times of the year, but the only really dangerous animals around here are the two-legged variety, humans, and the occasional wild boar. Of course I haven't mentioned spiders. I'm sure you're not scared of anything that has eight legs."

Cassie shuddered at the thought of her arachnophobic nightmares. "I haven't seen any people around. Are you expecting anyone to be here?"

He looked grim. "Yeah. Some people should turn up. When they arrive, stay out of sight. I don't want them to see who I've got tucked away in my bush shelter."

"Are your friends as primitive and uncivilized as you?"

"Worse. We're a little short on women out here."

Without thinking she moved a little closer to his broad frame. "Then I better keep out of sight, like you said."

"A lot depends on whether you're still here when they come."

"I hope I'm not going to be here that long."

"You could be." His stomach clenched at the thought of her leaving. It would be both heaven and hell for him, but he knew she would be itching to get away inside a week. In his experience city girls never stayed long in the country. And it would be better for her if she were gone, back to civilization.

"There's nothing here that would make me stay." Except you. The thought flashed into Cassie's mind with the force of nature. He alone could make her stay.

"How do you propose to leave?" Jack asked, as if it were of no concern to him at all.

"I can walk out of here to the nearest cattle station."

"It's a long way." Jack understood her look of frustration. Not getting what you wanted was hard to deal with. Anyway, in his opinion, civilization left a lot to be desired. He much preferred the clean fresh air of the outback.

"How do you get in contact with people?"

"I don't usually. Occasionally I get visitors but normally the only people I see are in Jasper Creek. Now and then I see stockmen, or prospectors. Sometimes Aborigines come. They know a lot about plants. It suits me just fine."

"You really are a hermit aren't you? Plants can't be the only reason to be out here." Cassie decided to get the question of why he was really there out in the open. "You're not hiding out here from the police are you?"

Jack acted like a man who didn't want to be found, a man with a murky past and uncertain future. She had no desire to be caught up in anything illegal, or dangerous.

He looked her straight in the eye. "You've got no idea the amount of people who want to get their hands on me."

Yes, I have she thought, looking over his hard muscular frame. She could feel her palms begin to tingle with anticipation and had to hold herself back.

He continued, "I stay here because that's the way I like it and I don't appreciate people coming here, telling me what I should or shouldn't do."

She could tell by the grim look on his face that she'd hit a nerve.

"I wouldn't dream of telling you what to do," she back-peddled. "I only want to know who I'm with. You could be a car salesman, or a serial killer. How would I know?"

"I never sell cars. I trade them in on better ones."

"So, maybe you're a politician hiding from his

constituents. I'm sure they wouldn't recognize you in what you're wearing. Your mother probably wouldn't either." She looked at his clothes. It was amazing they still held together.

"You're right about that. My mother wouldn't recognize me. She only sees me when I visit her in the city. I shave this beard off so she'll know me. I even put on a clean shirt, but the boots stay as they are."

Cassie looked at his mud caked boots and wrinkled her nose. "Welded on are they?"

"Absolutely."

"You're impossible. I never know when you're pulling my leg."

"If I do that, Cassie, believe me you'll know."

"Can't you at least tell me what to expect if those people come to see you?"

"Just be alert. If I say get out of sight, do it. It could be dangerous if you're seen." Jack looked deadly serious. "Some men can't be trusted."

"I know that. I'll do whatever has to be done." Cassie refused to admit she didn't feel confident in the wilderness any more, but she knew that if you gave any man an inch, he'd consider it his right to take that extra mile. It was the nature of the beast.

"You better believe one thing, I won't let anything happen to you."

The promise in his voice warned her of his basic approach to life, his need to be in control. It also told her of his caring nature. She believed he would pull her out of harm's way, even at a cost to his own life. It was that belief that made her trust him, and taunt him. "What about accidents. Mosquitoes can sting anyone. Me, or you." She wasn't sure a mosquito would dare bite that firm brown skin. It would break its proboscis.

"Mosquitoes have to take their best shot. I've got protection."

"What? A can of repellent?"

"No. A fast right hand." He clapped his hands together, disposing of an imaginary threat with the speed of light. "The left one needs work. I'm not ambidextrous, yet."

"I can't believe it. Something you aren't good at! There's hope for you yet, Jack."

Cassie grinned as she turned to walk away, but deep inside she was worried. She was unsure of how she would get home. Soberly, she took his warnings to heart. He was expecting company, people who might be trouble. Criminals perhaps. Keeping out of sight shouldn't be too difficult. She could always climb a tree or hide behind rocks.

She realized she would never be able to walk to the town of Jasper Creek, and there was no transport available. She was well and truly stuck here in the sole company of this Goliath of a man who acted and appeared like an advertisement in Vagrant's Weekly. There appeared to be no easy solution.

Cassie was just grateful he showed no real interest in her as a woman. That would have been too much for her to handle. She might have found herself responding, and that would never do. Her parents would have a major problem with it, and she would have...what would she have? An experience; or maybe something more? There would be no protection for her if she ended up in his arms.

When they finally reached Jack's camp, Cassie knew that her worst fears had not covered what lay before her. The term primitive was a gross exaggeration. It was more than primitive. It was prehistoric. The man who beckoned her forward had once again astonished her. How could a human being live like this? The makeshift tent, made of hessian bags sewn together, hung over fallen tree branches with bark over the top, was an eye opener. He called it a tent, and she supposed it was, of a sort. She was just grateful he wasn't living in a cave, wearing animal skins, and holding a club. Translating 'ug' into English was beyond her.

Three

♡

DUSK arrived swiftly, the sun sinking into the distant blue hills, leaving a cooling breeze to freshen the air. Cassie watched the sky fade, thinking it was strange to see the land as blue-gray, not the vivid terracotta of the daytime, or the brilliant colors of the setting sun. Alice Springs seemed a lifetime away. Nevada was even further.

Dozing before the campfire, listening to the night chorus, she waited for Jack. He strode into camp, dark hair long and scruffy, his beard dark with a reddish tinge, shabby khaki shorts, and an old army jacket.

She watched him remove his hat and grin, showing perfect white teeth and a cheeky glint in his eyes, and she didn't trust him, not one bit, not yet. Or perhaps the truth was that she didn't trust herself. The Aussie bush bandit confronting her was a whole new experience for a girl from the USA. As she got to know him, he seemed to change from a silent stranger into a man with infinite possibilities. This place seemed to relax him. Whenever he was with her she found herself waiting for his smile.

Watching as he opened a can of Irish stew, she realized she would have to be wary. He could sneak past her defenses, and she might find herself looking for more than his smile. She already knew he was attractive in a primitive kind of way, was sure when he had cleaned himself up, changing those disreputable shorts for something a little more respectable, he would be devastating.

Jack passed her an enamel plate filled with stew. He sat down opposite to eat his own meal, his voice deep and smooth as he said, "Sorry, we're out of wine. Water okay?"

"Yes, thanks." Cassie watched him in the flickering firelight, unconsciously moistening her lips, seeing the firm skin of his well-muscled arms flex tautly as he reached for the water. He really was a superb specimen of manhood she thought, great legs and taut...oops, she nearly choked on her food when he stood up and came around the fire towards her, moving like a jungle cat.

She was as still as a mouse while she waited for those long, strong legs to come within touching distance. And she suddenly wanted to touch him, badly. It was something she had no experience of, this craving of the flesh. Her world changed at that moment, giving her a glimpse of what she was missing out on by retreating from relationships as she had. She had let her insecurities control her life.

Jack had seen Cassie's nervous reaction to his movements, and as he reached her, handing her the tin cup of water, he searched her face for a reason. He hoped she was as aware of him as he was of her, his eyes darkening in appreciation of her delicate but earthy beauty in the flickering firelight. She was made for passion. He wanted to be around when she discovered its power for herself.

As Cassie looked into Jack's eyes, that power was revealed to her, and she trembled, suddenly overwhelmed by the hunger of the senses that he had awakened in her. She accepted the water, carefully not allowing their hands to touch, looking away from Jack's questioning eyes, turning from the temptation he offered, denying her own needs.

He smiled the patient smile of the tiger and returned to his seat by the fire, content to wait. He knew the value of allowing his quarry a chance to regain lost confidence. She deserved a chance to become the hunter, to test her strength. All he needed was time to sort out his problems, and then he would come for her. The drawback was, would she still be there? Waiting? And would she want him when he came? Only time would tell.

"Jack, I'd like to ask you something."

"You can ask? Doesn't mean I'll answer."

"Will you take me to Alcoota. I don't mind walking, but going alone is hazardous."

"No." Jack was back to one-syllable words.

"Why not? You seem to be going in that direction?"

"I wasn't going up that far."

"But Jack, I have to get there before the wet season starts. The creeks will fill up. Fossils will sink in the mud. Can't you see how important it is to me?"

"Yes, but I can't take you. It's too far to walk, and I haven't got time to spare. I have things happening right now that I can't ignore. Sorry, but it's out of my hands."

Cassie looked at him with hurt in her eyes. "All right. If that's your decision. Maybe in Jasper Creek I can hire another vehicle. Surely that's not too far?"

"Go to sleep, Cassie. Forget about going to Alcoota for now."

Jack turned away from her, walking off into the trees. When he returned a few minutes later, he put his sleeping bag on the other side of the fire and lay down. He didn't speak, just closed his eyes.

All she could do was fume silently, thinking up words to describe him, words she would never speak aloud. She had to do something to distract herself, something necessary. "I'm going to find my own bathroom, Jack. If I don't come back in ten minutes, come find me, but don't turn the flashlight on."

Cassie disappeared behind some trees, leaving Jack wondering what he would do if she decided to leave. How could he stop her? She was a free woman. She was also extremely vulnerable. If she stayed, there could be danger for her. If she left, there could also be trouble. Either way, he thought, it was a problem, but keeping her close was what he needed to do. What he wanted to do was another story. It involved moving his sleeping bag to her side of the fire and letting nature take its course.

Cassie returned then and Jack shifted uncomfortably, grateful for the darkness.

He hadn't talked much since they had met, so she surmised that he was used to living alone and wasn't about to chat to any pesky female who happened to come along. In that respect, he reminded her of her father and brothers. They also believed her to be a nuisance, a pest to be tolerated, but controlled. That was why she had to fight to be free. She had always hated cages, and wasn't about to be put in one for any reason.

Days of walking had taken their toll on Cassie, so she moved into the shelter. Sleep came in the middle of an impossible idea to hike back to Plenty Highway.

Well into the night Jack woke up to feed the fire, always conscious of the responsibility he had taken on when he had brought Cassie with him.

He had to protect her but, as his hand touched the cold metal of his rifle by his side, he hoped it wouldn't be necessary to use it for anything other than hunting for food.

The rest of his night was spent in restless anticipation of the day ahead, knowing always that Cassie was close by, realizing that what he was beginning to want from her he might never be able to have.

Cassie woke suddenly from a deep sleep, hearing what she thought was a vehicle backfiring. Unfortunately it wasn't. The explosive flash of lightning was followed by the crack of a large gum tree snapping in two. The storm Jack had predicted had arrived in all its fury.

Rain hurtled down from the sky in torrents, the run-off flowing along a groove in the ground, through the shelter on its way down the hill. It was surprisingly dry inside the makeshift sanctuary. Cassie realized that between the hessian bags and bark was a large piece of canvas.

The structure started shaking as a large creature threw itself in through the opening. Shaggy hair was thrown back from a wet face, showing a bedraggled specimen that could have doubled for Bigfoot. It was growling, cursing the elements with great imagination. Cassie would have applauded, but Jack suddenly stripped off his shirt and grabbed the spare blanket from the foot of Cassie's sleeping bag. Shivering, he wrapped himself up, toeing off his boots at the same time.

"What the hell are you doing?" she asked, although what he was doing was obvious.

"Bloody weather. I didn't expect it this quick." He added, "It's wet out there."

"Really?" she said with irritating sarcasm. "I wouldn't have known."

Jack had lost his tact with the first trail of cold water in his sleeping bag. "Too busy sleeping in my tent, are you? Come outside and feel the rain. It's your wake-up call."

"I would have slept somewhere else if you'd asked."

Warily, she watched him take another groundsheet from a box of supplies.

"Then you would have been drenched instead of me. Either way ends up the same, we share."

"You're not getting in my sleeping bag." Her protest was instant.

"I would if I could. At least you're warm." Jack grinned and her mistrust doubled. "Relax. I'm talking about sharing the tent, not the sleeping bag."

Cassie realized she had no choice. "Just so long as you stay on your side."

Jack frowned at her nervous tone. Surely she didn't think she was in danger from him. "You aren't scared of me are you, Cassie?"

"No, of course not," she asserted, a thread of doubt finding it's way along her vocal chords. "I just don't want to get wet." To her relief he seemed to believe her and turned away. "So, are you going to stay in here all night?" she asked.

"Where else would I sleep?" He looked at her over his shoulder, one eyebrow raised.

"In a hollow log," she suggested hopefully.

"Would you like to go out and find me one?"

She looked out at the rain, bucketing down in the darkness, and shuddered. "No way. You can stay here, until it stops."

"That's what I thought." He grinned.

Cassie knew when it was time to keep her mouth shut. She'd suffer the impossible situation until the next day when, rain or not, she'd start walking to a main road and hitch a ride to somewhere. Jasper Creek would do. Surely there'd be a truck going that way?

Cassie awoke at dawn to find she was alone. She dragged her aching body out into daylight. The ground underfoot was soggy with red mud, rivulets flowing along tracks channeled out during the deluge. The rain had stopped for now, leaving the air cool but refreshing.

Cassie yearned for a hot drink but she'd have to wait until the temperature rose and the wood dried out. She was standing outside the shelter, looking out over the flooded landscape, shivering, when Jack returned a few minutes later. He came up the side of the hill where the undergrowth was thickest, keeping his foothold on the slippery slope.

"How could it flood so quickly?" she asked.

"Haven't you ever been in Australia when it rains?"

"Yes, I have, but I haven't seen a downpour like this. Will the floodwaters keep rising? I don't want to be stuck here?"

"Water won't go much higher. There shouldn't be any more rain for a while."

"I want to get out of here, Jack?" Cassie willed her voice to stay steady.

"I know you do." Jack seemed to sense her hidden fears, and she hated that he could read her so well. Her self-protective layers were crumbling before her eyes.

He said, "I don't know how far the flood has spread. We could be trapped until the waters recede." She gasped in dismay and, softening his tone, he tried to reassure her. "On the other hand, we could get out of here in a few days if the rain holds off."

"What are we going to do? I can probably go to Alcoota next year, but now I should try to get out and call home. Mom and Dad could be frantic. They might see this flood on the cable weather channel. World news might have it on. That sometimes covers Australia. I haven't talked to them for a week, but they know the general area I planned to visit."

"Nothing we can do, Cassie. No power, no phone, no transport. It's relatively safe here though, so we'll just have to make the best of a bad situation."

"How do we do that? We'll run out of food long before anyone realizes where we are." She glared at him, her frustration at his seeming complacency fuelling her temper.

"Trust me, I've a bit of experience at this. We'll manage."

"But there isn't anything here. We're on a hill in the middle of a sea of water."

Cassie thought of her comfortable life back home, protected, and secure. She hadn't wanted to be safe, surrounded by her family, caged by work commitments, but now it looked like heaven.

She had always been able to do as she pleased, but this time she was trapped in a situation not of her choosing. She didn't like it at all. The fact that Jack was stranded too only added to her discomfort. Her reactions to him were startling and she didn't like that either. Her independence was in danger of being seriously undermined.

Added to that were her recurring fantasies about being stranded on a desert island with a handsome pirate. She cursed all the historical romances she had ever read. They were coming back to haunt her in a way she had never dreamed.

"We won't starve," he assured her, oblivious to the tumult of her thoughts. "There are always rabbits that find dry ground in a flood." He deliberately didn't mention the snakes, not being sure of her reaction. Hysteria he didn't need at this point in time. "We'll set up a snare. Anyway, not all the ground will be flooded; there could be a way through to a deserted mining area on the other side of this hill. I've been down that road a few years ago. It's steep and rocky. We'd have a hard climb."

"Where does it end up?"

"Back at the Plenty Highway. I'm not sure how far we'd get before we hit more floods. This area is strewn with creeks and rivers that only flow in the wet season."

"You don't seem to care that we could starve, or drown." Cassie felt as though her hands were tied and wanted to scream.

"I'll find some dry wood to light a fire. We'll be okay."

Cassie sat near to Jack on one of his makeshift log seats, hunching her shoulders against the cold. "I wish your cell phone would work. Then at least we could tell someone where we are. Hey, what about smoke signals?"

"You've been watching too much cable TV. Look at it this way, at least we'll get to know each other." He laughed at the look of horror that crossed her expressive face. "Doesn't that appeal to your ladyship?"

"Not particularly, but I suppose I don't have a choice." She glared balefully at his cheerful grin. He really had the weirdest sense of humor. She didn't think the situation was funny at all. And neither would her family. They would consider the whole thing reprehensible and totally her fault. Her mother would probably deliver one of her lectures. Cassie would pretend to ignore it, as usual. Her dad would advise her to look at the weather forecast before she left the house. As if that could have prevented the rain!

Jack stood up and announced, "I'm going to have a look around. I'll be back before nightfall."

Even though Cassie was unsure about him, she began to feel lonely as soon as he'd gone. She wished she hadn't left her cell phone in the jeep. Consoling herself, she thought, Jack's right. It probably wouldn't have worked out here anyway. Too many hills, and not a strong enough signal.

She shivered as she contemplated the water surrounding them. The reason he'd placed his camp on the hill was clear. He must have known the water would rise here. Cassie was grateful; they could have drowned if they'd been down on the flat area.

She wondered if the water had reached to where her jeep had been abandoned? It'd be just her luck if the flood washed it away, and she never saw it again. Good thing she took out insurance. At least that was something she'd done right.

Jack returned two hours later with something in a hessian bag. He smiled secretively, "I found our lunch. You better go for a walk while I cook it."

"Don't be silly, Jack, I'm not squeamish. I know we have to eat. Let me see."

"Oh, all right. But remember, beggars can't be choosers." He pulled the bag open and put his hand in.

Cassie waited, her chest tight, to see what he'd caught, perhaps a rabbit or a fish? Her stomach was growling loudly, her mouth watering, as she drew from memory the smell of campfire cooking a stew. Delicious.

The snake he produced brought her heart into her throat. Imagining she saw the tail move, she couldn't even scream. He held it out to her and said, "Hold it for me, Cassie. I'll get my knife."

Cassie turned bilious green and fled to the other side of the clearing. Jack could hear her taking deep breaths. "You okay?" he asked, struggling to keep a straight face. There was nothing quite like being tossed in at the deep end.

"No. I'm not." She glared at him as she came closer.

"And I'm certainly not going to eat snake. Is it dead? I saw the tail move."

"It's not breathing," he said cheerfully, putting it up to his ear. "That's all I could find for us. I swished it around in the river, so it's clean."

"I'd rather starve, thank you very much."

"You probably will." He grinned at her outrage. "Let me know if you change your mind. I'll save some for you. I call it snake steak. A bush delicacy. Lots of protein."

"Don't bother. I'll go and find my own food, rabbit or fish, or something."

"Go for it. I'd love to see you catch a rabbit with your bare hands." Jack grinned mockingly as he attended to the snake.

"I'm quick on my feet, I reckon I could catch anything if I felt like it."

"Reality check, Cassie. If I was a rabbit you'd call me bugs and give me a carrot."

"If you were a rabbit, I'd catch you by the ears and make you into rabbit stew so fast your head would spin." She looked him up and down and laughed. "I'm glad you're not a rabbit though."

"Oh, why is that?"

"Because I really prefer fish. May I borrow that fishing line I saw in your camp?"

"Sure, but if you catch anything you have to share."

Cassie was heading away down the path when Jack said, "Don't forget to keep an eye out for other kinds of snakes. There are several varieties around here that are extremely deadly."

"I haven't seen any so far."

"They usually disappear when they sense someone's coming. The ground vibrates and they pick up on that."

Cassie's skin tingled as she thought of the danger

around her. "Is there anything out here that isn't dangerous?"

"I think I'm fairly harmless." He grinned, and she knew it was a lie.

"That's a matter of opinion. Isn't man supposed to be the most dangerous predator?"

"I hope you include women in that sweeping statement."

Cassie laughed. "Yeah. Women are even more deadly than the male, so watch out." She looked at the snake and frowned. "That looks disgusting. I'm going to find something else to eat. Something that doesn't slither on my plate."

She left the camp without another word, wanting to catch a fish, cook and eat it in front of him. And gloat. Not an attractive trait but human nonetheless. Gloating only works when you've got an escape route. She didn't.

Purposefully, she avoided the long grasses by the edge of the water in case a reptile might see her as his next meal. She headed over the hill to where Jack had said there was high ground.

Cassie disappeared from sight. Jack decided to give her a few minutes before following. This compulsion to be with her had him confused. It wasn't the way he usually behaved. Whenever a woman had started to get too close to him in the past, he retreated into his work. Over the years it had become a habit to avoid anyone who would put pressure on him to socialize.

Even his parents and sister had given up on him; he was accepted as a perennial bachelor. The fact that he was a fantastic catch for any woman was something he was oblivious to. There were other things in life to grab his attention, namely his work.

Women seemed to want him. He rarely felt strongly

enough about any of them to want them in return, until now. Jack liked them as friends and that was all.

Deciding he wasn't going to let Cassie get to him, he deliberately sat down and started sorting through his pack, making notes in his journal. He assured himself that it was only natural to look at his watch every few minutes.

It was almost an hour later when Jack realized he'd been on the edge of his seat, listening for sounds of Cassie returning. His notebook had fallen to the ground, his attention to his work lost, something that had never happened before.

He took the snake from the spiked stick he had skewered it with for cooking, wrapping it in cloth to protect it from flies. Then he walked to the top of the hill, searching the area with keen eyes. He found nothing. To be on the safe side, Jack went to get his rifle, stashed under some hessian bags in the shelter.

Concerned, more than worried, Jack slid down the hill and walked through some straggly trees toward a rocky outcrop near the water's edge. He could see Cassie hadn't come that way, so he turned towards the next hill, squelching his way through the mud and sword grass along the bank.

Bush flies buzzed around him, he brushed them away impatiently. They'd carry a man away if they could. Then he heard a strange sound coming from a gum tree. He froze, his sharp eyes searching, finding the source of the guttural squealing. A wild boar was grunting and fussing in the bushes at the base of the tree.

They could be extremely dangerous, their tusks able to rip a man in one swipe, so he trod warily. Instantly, something else caught his eye. It was Cassie, clinging to a branch with one arm, waving with the other.

Jack swallowed convulsively, the fear he felt for her

rising in his throat. He crept closer through rocks and bushes, oblivious to the branches that scratched at his bare arms and drew blood. He had to be careful not to startle the beast into rushing him. He was no good to anyone if he became a corpse.

"Jack." Cassie shivered as he came closer. "Be careful. This pig has enormous tusks." Cassie's fear had shifted from herself to Jack. Better to be stuck in the tree forever than have Jack injured or killed. This concern for his safety was not something she thought about. It was deep in her subconscious.

He waved to her so she'd know he'd seen and heard her, giving a thumbs up signal. As the boar snuffled under the tree, his snout in the dirt, Jack lifted the rifle to his shoulder and took aim. He rarely used it, but this was an emergency, he could see no other way of removing the dangerous creature from under the tree.

The boar turned toward him as he sighted down the barrel. It broke into a run, squealing, the primal instinct to protect its territory overwhelming, and its power awesome. He fired once, killing it instantly. Jack hated killing things, regretting that, sometimes, in cases of danger or hunger it became necessary. He walked over to the carcass thinking, how the hell am I going to get it back to camp?

Cassie had no idea that Jack regretted the necessity of disposing of the boar. She was elevating him to hero status, even while her nerves were jumping in reaction. "Are you sure it's dead?" she asked, as she climbed down from the safety of the tree branch. Jack held his breath a she swung momentarily from a branch, and then let go.

"What do you think?" He prodded the boar with his foot.

"I don't know do I? It looks dead. Where did that blood on your shirt come from?"

"It's hard to say." Jack hadn't noticed the blood. He was too busy checking the area for more wild pigs.

Cassie was rapidly losing patience. She valiantly tried again, speaking slowly as if he were deaf. "Why is it hard to say Jack, surely you'd know if you were injured or not?"

The strain was beginning to tell, her voice was tense.

"Yeah, I'd know."

When no words were forthcoming she said explosively, "Damn it, Jack, tell me where the blood is coming from or I'll hit you."

"No need to get violent, Cassie."

"I feel violent. Talk to me, damn it."

He shrugged. "Look, don't fuss. I've got a couple of scratches that are leaking a bit, nothing to get steamed up about. The pig is the one with the problem."

She looked at the corpse and shuddered. "He doesn't have a problem any more."

"I'm glad I had my rifle with me," he said. "We could have both been in trouble. These tusks are deadly."

"Do you think there are any more of them?"

"Probably quite a few, but they generally stay away from people. As you said earlier, we're the predators out here."

"I've always felt uncomfortable with guns, but maybe I'd better get one, just in case."

Jack looked sternly at Cassie, "Even if you did have a rifle, it would have attacked before you could figure out how to pull the trigger."

"I can do anything you can do."

"Do you reckon you'd be able to use a weapon in self-defense?"

"Sure I would," she said, a defiant glint in her eye.

He grinned. "I'll believe it when I see it."

"You'd be surprised at what I can do when I'm pushed, Jack."

"Well then, if you can do anything a man can do, you can carry the boar back to camp." Jack heaved the blood soaked carcass into his arms and brought it over to her, tossing it down at her feet. He didn't say it was heavy. He had no need to.

She jumped back involuntarily. "No thanks. I'll leave that honor to you."

"Okay, I'll carry it, but you can do the rest."

"What would that be?"

"It needs to be cleaned and gutted. And cut up. Then you have to cook it."

"No way."

"I thought you could tackle anything that a man could, and do a better job as well."

"Well, perhaps I was a tiny bit mistaken. But this is the only time. Anyway butchers are always men. It's tradition."

"You're sure of that?" He looked at her with disbelief in his eyes.

"Of course I'm sure." She said hastily, "I'll get the fire going. I'm really hungry."

"I take it you didn't catch a fish?"

"I didn't get to the water. The pig found me first."

"I'm hungry too, Cassie. But not for food." There was something about hunting that brought out the beast in men. Jack was no exception. Must be the smell of blood, he thought, wanting nothing more than to toss her over his shoulder, and ...

His imagination stalled as Cassie asked, "What then?" She saw the look in his eyes, suddenly realizing what he meant. A blush slowly crept up her cheeks, and she turned away, embarrassed. "Forget I asked," she muttered.

Jack looked like the predator he had mentioned earlier. Hunger and need were in his eyes as he watched her. Cassie wanted to run, even while she wanted to stay and find out what he had in mind.

Sensing her need for flight, Jack was amazed at her innocence. It was unusual, and he was elated that it was so, having discovered a proprietary streak in himself for her. She was such a little spitfire with her aggressively independent spirit. She'd probably give a black eye to any guy who tried to take what she didn't want to give. With a possessive feeling that gave him a start of surprise, that thought pleased him immensely.

Jack wrapped his scratched arm with a handkerchief, and tied the feet of the beast with a piece of baling twine he had in his pocket. It was handy for tying fresh food up in a tree when he was on the trail. He then heaved the boar onto his shoulders, saying, "Let's go. Carry the rifle could you, Cassie?"

Cassie retrieved the fishing line and picked up the rifle. "Is it loaded?"

"Not any more. It would be too much of a risk having you walk behind me with a loaded gun." He chuckled at her look of resentment. "You might be hungry enough to finish me off and keep all the pork spare-ribs for yourself."

"Don't tempt me."

Jack wished he could but that might be stretching it a bit. "If you want to eat, you have to help cook."

Gritting her teeth at his bossy tone, Cassie started back to camp with Jack, carrying the gun, wishing for the hundredth time that she had brought a larger supply of pre-packed food with her. What they had was for emergency use only. It's no use crying for the moon, she thought resignedly. I'd better help cook the pig, no matter how much I hate doing it. After all, we have to eat.

When they arrived back at camp, Cassie turned to Jack. "Okay, let me have a look at that sore arm. It'll be easier if I do it."

"You're fussing again, Cassie. I told you, it's just a simple scratch."

"For goodness sake, put the damn pig down. I want to disinfect your arm."

"Playing nurse, are we?" he mocked. When she scowled, he said, "Oh, all right. But don't take too long about it. There's a whole platoon of flies ready to land on this porker." He sat on a log and stripped off his shirt. The first aid kit was in his pack.

The scratch was long but not deep, so Cassie simply cleaned it with disinfectant before wrapping it in a bandage. "There you go, macho man. Didn't hurt a bit did it?"

"Course not," he growled, putting his shirt back on. "I've got work to do, the pig's waiting. You might like to get that fire going." He tossed her a packet of matches.

Cassie watched Jack get out his knife to attack the pig's carcass, thinking, it wouldn't hurt you to say 'thank you, Cassie'. No, that would be too much to expect. Still, he did look rather magnificent, a hunter taking care of business, providing food for his family, his woman. Where had that thought come from? She wasn't his woman. Even though she wished…whatever she wished was forgotten as he shouted, "You got that fire going yet? I'm almost ready." So am I she thought. So am I.

Four

If you took away the memory of it being slaughtered, Cassie decided that wild pork wasn't too bad. Unfortunately, she had an excellent memory for details. She decided again to bring dried food if they ever returned to this spot. It was the only way to go.

With a sense of shock, she realized that she had been including Jack when she thought of coming here again. Why did she do that, she asked herself indignantly? As soon as she reached civilization he'd be out of her life, more than likely, and she'd never see him again. She'd be home in Nevada with her fossils. He'd be here, looking for plants. Unaccountably the thought made her scowl.

Later that evening Cassie got the first aid supplies and headed toward Jack. "Would you like me to clean and bandage your arm again?"

He was surprised, having forgotten about it, replying gruffly, "It's nothing."

"You're the one who said be careful because in this climate scratches could become serious infections." Her cool gaze cut though his defenses, leaving him without excuse.

"I know I said that, but I meant you, not a guy like me."

"A tough guy you mean? You are human aren't you? You bleed like anyone else?"

His eyes took on a sleepy look as he took in her small, exotic shape in slim fitting jeans and loose shirt. She wriggled like a worm on a hook when that gaze reached her rounded breasts, and lingered with deliberate assessment.

"Oh yes, I find that I'm quite human," he purred throatily. "In fact I would go so far as to say my flesh is incredibly weak and vulnerable at this moment."

He stripped off his shirt, exposing his tanned body to her startled gaze. She had only wanted his arm, not the whole box and dice. Be careful what you wish for, her mother had told her. Now she knew what that advice meant. Hands trembling, she laid the cotton wool, gauze and antiseptic out on her lap, and proceeded to clean his scratches.

Being impersonal about it was getting harder by the minute. How is it, she wondered, that supple tanned skin and muscular arms have such a devastating effect on me? Surely one man is the same as another? What makes this one so different?

Slowly, she stroked the antiseptic across the wound. Was he purring? Was she? She'd seen tigers at zoos with the same sensual concentration on pleasure.

It was mesmeric, the way she felt when she touched his naked skin, like a vibration zinging through her blood stream. Her throat dried, her skin became clammy, as he flexed his arm so she could reach right around. She gulped air, moistening her lips in a desperate attempt to appear normal, lest he notice her agitation.

She looked up, finding his concentrated gaze on her hands. Wondering what he saw, she looked down. Her fingers were moving over his naked flesh in a slow, sensual, dance of seduction, stroking, forward and back, up and down. Heat overwhelmed her. It suddenly became imperative to divert his attention. Briskly efficient, she rapidly bandaged his arm, saying, "I think you'll live. But no more pig hunting, okay?"

Jack's voice was hoarse "I can't promise I'll never hunt again. Next time I'll go to your place. I can hunt alligators instead. Does that suit you Miss Nightingale?"

Cassie forced herself to stop looking at rippling muscles. "Don't expect me to sew your leg back on after it's been chewed off by some prehistoric reptile. I'm going to bed. Goodnight, Jack." She picked up the first aid supplies and turned to go.

"Yes, go to bed, Cassie," he advised, his voice rich with amusement. "Sleep well. The only reptiles around here are snakes that are looking for warmth. They sometimes creep into sleeping bags."

When she glared back at him, he added softly, "Males are attracted to warmth too."

"Ah, yes. Men. The real predators." Turning, she escaped, before he found a reply.

It was late afternoon the next day, the heat gradually lowering in temperature, when Cassie said casually, "Jack, do you think there's going to be any more rain?"

"Possibly. A bit hard to tell right now. Why?"

"I was wondering whether you could sleep by the fire tonight?"

He looked at her suspiciously and she went on, "I mean, the tent, I presume you call it a tent, it isn't very big." Not big! She nearly choked on the words. He was practically sleeping on top of her.

"I had noticed," he said dryly. "Come on, spit it out before it chokes you."

"All right. I want you to sleep out of the tent because I need some privacy. I'm not used to sharing a room." She wasn't used to breathing the same air, night after night, with a man either. If she didn't get some sleep soon, she'd fall over.

"Your snoring doesn't bother me; if that's what's worrying you?"

"I don't snore," she asserted. "I don't sleep! Not with you in my tent."

"Your tent?" He laughed. "Who built that thing from the ground up? Yours truly."

"Damn it Jack, couldn't you pretend to be a gentleman for once? It's not as if you're not used to spending nights outside, sleeping rough."

"Yeah, right, but if it rains, I'll be back. In the meantime, I'll see if I can be gentleman enough to allow you to go first for a proper wash. Be careful though; don't forget the porker that went after you. There could be others around. And snakes."

"Great. Just what I needed to hear." She glared at his mocking grin, heading off, hoping to avoid a confrontation with more feral creatures.

Down at the water's edge, Cassie absorbed the stillness of the early evening. She had always loved the close of day when birds seemed to do a final round before settling down for the night. Bugs and worms probably did the same, that could be the attraction.

The hustle and bustle of the city no longer existed, all that mattered was the freedom to listen, and feel at one with nature. Australia was a land where even the smallest creature's life was of value, where the largest creatures had once lived, where kangaroos still roamed. She had hoped to camp along dry riverbeds, digging for fossils, but now it had rained that wouldn't be possible. Mud would quickly stake its claim.

She sighed despondently; perhaps next year when she had saved more money, she'd be able to return to the MacDonnell Ranges. Cassie had a flash of her parent's reaction and knew she would have a hard time convincing them of her ability to keep herself safe. She loved her family but they wanted to keep her in a cage. She often found herself rejecting their opinions, even before they made them known.

She could envisage the scene as her brothers contributed their advice as well, and was glad she was old enough to decide for herself. She wondered what they would think of Jack? Not much she thought. Not being American, he wouldn't be considered right for her. He was casual, relaxed, confident, and Cassie decided she liked him that way. He didn't need the trappings of civilization to make him a desirable man.

The problem was, what did he think of her? Since he was short on conversation, long on action, how was she ever to find out? Maybe she could give him a tiny push in the right direction? It wasn't unfair; girls back home did it all the time.

Sometimes they win, sometimes they lose, whispered a soft voice in her mind. Do you want to take that chance? As she took off her clothes and slipped naked into the water, she still didn't have an answer. And if she didn't get him out of the tent, the whole thing could be taken right out of her hands.

Jack fed some wood to the fire before sitting back on his heels. The water should recede in three or four days he thought, wondering what they were going to do until then. Not what he wanted to do, that was for sure. She wanted him to move out of the tent, that was a clear indication of her rejection. She was saying no, in no uncertain terms. Trouble was, he couldn't remember having asked a question.

No, he taunted himself; you just look at her as though she's your next meal. She doesn't want to be devoured by someone living in the desert like a hobo. She needs a man in a civilized suit, a man with a haircut, and a bank account. I've got that, he assured himself, rebuilding his confidence; you just can't see any evidence of it.

He wished they'd made it to his camp further north, but it wasn't worth the danger of tackling the flood to get to it. Easier to wait until the water soaked into the earth, then walk out to the highway and hitch a lift to Jasper Creek. Once there he could send Cassie on her way and get back to his work.

At the other camp, he had his own SUV pickup truck, but with the floods, the roads would still be cut off, making it impossible to drive out. Getting bogged in deep mud in a vehicle that size was no picnic, even with a winch and a tree to attach it to.

When Cassie arrived back, she said, "Your turn to scrub, Jack. You better hurry though, it's getting dark and cold." She grinned at him as he stood and, gathering his things, started down the hill. She called after him, "Don't let the dingoes get you. Remember, they eat meat." And that's something you've got a lot of, she thought, admiring his wide shoulders as he walked away. No shortage of protein there.

"Did you see dingoes down at the water?" Jack turned back at her words, interested when she mentioned Australia's wild dog. He had studied them at every opportunity.

"No, but I remember you said they could dangerous."

"I always respect animals in the wild. Don't worry, girl. They'd probably take one look at your red hair and decide that carrots weren't part of their diet."

That was too much for Cassie. "At least I wouldn't have given them indigestion. Someone as big as you would give them a week of meals in one go." What a feast she thought, unconsciously licking her lips as she looked her fill.

Jack refused to dignify that comment with a reply and had turned away, not noticing the look she was giving him. He quickly slid down the slope towards the water, making plans to tame that copper-headed smart aleck and make her eat her words about his size. He couldn't wait to show her that he was all muscle, not pale flab like her city boyfriends probably were.

He'd developed an impressive array of muscles in his thirty-one years. Reserve army training had built his stamina to the point where he could compete with most athletes and come out a winner. He thought of all the hours that he spent working, digging in the desert for rare plants, using only his hands and a shovel, walking through the bush. If he hadn't developed muscles with all that exercise, there would have been something seriously wrong.

When Jack reached the water there were signs that it was receding. Trees were surfacing, birds were landing, and mud could be seen at the edge of the water.

He took off his boots and socks, shedding his clothes in the warm, evening air, reveling in the freedom of movement. Then he walked slowly into the cool, soothing water, swimming against the current a little way upstream.

He used strong, powerful strokes, skillfully matching the current's strength. He trod water, apparently unaware of the eyes that watched and waited for him to emerge from the swirling flow.

When he drifted back to the place where he had entered the water, Jack stood up and waded through the shallows. He bent, dipped his head in the water then reached for the soap he had left on the bank. He soaped his mane of hair and the rest of his body with economic movements, and then dived back into the water.

His shoulders emerged moments later, and he shook his hair out of his eyes as water streamed from his body. Rays of golden light from the dying sun flowed across the rippling water, highlighting the planes and hollows of Jack's upper body with a fiery glow. The helplessly enthralled girl watching him moved restlessly as a strangely hollow feeling was made known. Guilt rode her hard, but she could not stop her gaze following him. He would never know, was her excuse.

She began to feel warm deep inside as he turned away, lifting his face to the setting sun like a pagan supplicant, moving his hands up to smooth his shoulder length hair away from his face, his shoulders flexing, his muscles stirring under supple skin.

After a few moments he turned once again and walked towards her, out of the water. The towel he had taken with him was used to absorb moisture, and then casually slung over his shoulder while he bent to pull on his shorts. He gathered up his things, starting back to camp in the gathering twilight, and she breathed once more.

As Jack climbed back up the hill to camp, Cassie hurried back too, disappearing into the tent, ashamed of her voyeurism, knowing it could become a habit. She had wanted to look at the sunset from her vantage point on the hill, but it had taken second place to the man who was becoming her obsession.

She hadn't meant to spy, but once she had glimpsed him swimming, she was held immobile by the beauty of his rhythm in the water. It was his natural element.

She emerged from the tent while Jack was lighting a fire, hoping he hadn't noticed her watching him. Trees surrounding their campsite had an eerie effect, the breeze rustling the leaves together. Cassie stoked the fire, placing branches on it, creating a warm glow. She was like a tightly wound spring, ready to break apart at the slightest movement.

In the cool evening air, the hot tea Jack produced was very welcome. Cassie was grateful he hadn't seen her on the hill, watching him, salivating. She mocked herself for the way her mouth had watered; she had never felt so hot in her life before. He had no knowledge of her visit to the vantage point or he would have said something, wouldn't he? It was a secret she would never reveal, not to anyone.

Flames were burning brightly and a good bed of coals was ready for food to be cooked. Jack sliced up some pork he'd kept cool in the river, and then he placed it in a saucepan. His supplies included packets of dried vegetables and sauces and soon the smell of spicy sweet and sour pork was wafting through the air, sending Cassie's taste buds into a spasm. Now she was salivating with a vengeance.

"Do you like cooking" he asked.

"Sure. When I get to choose what to cook."

"Ingrate," Jack accused, laughing. "Next time you catch the food and cook it as well."

"I tried to catch it. Didn't quite make it to the water. There was a pig in the way."

Jack could hardly think straight. He watched Cassie as firelight turned her hair to flame. He'd seen her on the hillside, watching him, but he would never tell her.

"The pig's history, Cassie," he said. "We had it for dinner."

"I realize that." She shook her head. "I'm going to bed now. Turn out the light will you?" She crawled into the tent, lying fully dressed on her sleeping bag. She had a plan for the next day, and wanted an early start.

Jack settled down by the fire and continued feeding it. He hoped it would rain so he could move into the tent with Cassie. All he needed was an excuse. It was the cry of a desperate man.

She was an intriguing mixture of innocence and woman of the world, and he was constantly battling the desire to touch her. Even the freckles on her nose were a great temptation to him. He wanted to count them, then see if there were any more to count that he hadn't noticed. He wondered what she would do if she knew of his other self, the man who lived another life, far away from this vast primeval land?

Finally the exertions of the day overcame Jack and he slept, wrapped in his sleeping bag by the dying fire. He didn't hear the small noises made as Cassie arose before dawn, gathering up her pack, heading away from the camp towards the distant hills.

The air was crisp and cool, the fragrance of wild flowers emerging from the earth a subtle hint of the glorious colors to be seen across the land. It was like an awakening, the spirit of the land at one with the spirit of the air, both flooding the senses with the knowledge of eternity.

The floodwaters had gone down considerably during the night. Cassie had decided to go her own way, as usual. She had a job to get back to and a family who would be worried about her. She also had Alcoota, and other paleontology projects to look forward to. Dinosaurs were beckoning. It was time to get her life back on track, and Jack wasn't part of it. He was just a fascinating diversion.

As she was leaving, Cassie took a last regretful look at the man lying peacefully by the embers of the campfire. He was a terrible temptation, but not for her. He was going in a completely different direction.

The sun was coming up as Cassie reached the first rocky outcrop. She looked back at the sky as she took a break. It was quite spectacular in its beauty, an artist's palette strewn with reds and yellows, mauves and blues, even a splash of green. She wished there was someone she could share it with. Jack's face swam into her mind, circling her memories, sharpening her regret. His dark lashed hazel eyes seemed to say, I could have shared this with you, but you didn't give me the chance.

He was an enigma. She wished she had time to solve the puzzle but it was not to be. Too many days had passed and she had to get back to Alice Springs, and then home to America.

Soon after midday Cassie paused to contemplate the river before her. It was swollen with the rain that had fallen and was now dangerously wide. She walked upstream until it became slightly narrower, easier to cross. She sat on the bank watching for a while before trying to wade across. A large rock midstream could be reached quite easily; she thought it would provide a convenient place to rest.

The risk wouldn't stop her. She wondered what Mike, her eldest brother, would do in the same situation. Would he take a chance, or would he stay safe. Mike was eight years older than Cassie, a geologist. He had been an adult by the time she was a teenager, out of her orbit since he had left home to attend university in California. He'd do it, she told herself, and he'd try to cross. Mike wasn't afraid of anything, least of all a stretch of muddy water. He would go for it without hesitation.

Cassie decided she could do no less than the males in her family. She removed her boots, tying them around her neck, placing her socks in her pack, which she hoisted onto her back.

Leaving arms free for balance, she stepped into the water. The current grabbed at her feet but it was not enough to sway her from the course she had chosen.

It was cool but not uncomfortable as Cassie stepped through the shallows, her shorts barely getting wet. Debris floated past, tree branches a danger, as she placed her feet carefully on the riverbed. It was strewn with stones.

She was up to her waist when she felt the water around her bare feet becoming colder; it was much deeper when she neared the rock, coming almost up to her chest. She reached out her hands, grabbing the smooth stone, anchoring herself midstream while she rested.

Spray flew when a breeze whipped up, making the rocks wet and cooling the air around her. After a few minutes clinging to the rock, legs floating into the current, Cassie was ready to complete her journey across the river. It was not without some trepidation that she began again, wishing all the while that she had never begun such a perilous journey, that she was safe back at camp with Jack. Only her stubborn will and her dislike of admitting defeat forced her to continue.

Cassie could see trees and dry land not too far away, and started off in a direct line to reach them. She was doing fine until her foot slipped on the smooth stones of the riverbed. She fell backwards. Within seconds she was totally submerged and being dragged downstream by the strong current. She surfaced, gasping painfully for air.

The water was deep. She panicked as she grabbed at a tree branch floating past. Leaves and sharp sticks stung her face when she tried to hang on in the rapidly moving water. She threw an arm up to protect herself. Another tree barreled past while she was struggling, clipping her a glancing blow on the head.

Dizziness overcame her. She lost her grip, swallowing quite a bit of muddy river water, coughing and retching. The pain in her head was like hot needles as the violently swirling water swamped her, tumbling out of control. Her strength was drained, she felt helpless as she submerged, again and again, kicking her legs and flailing her arms in an attempt to stay afloat. She didn't think she was going to die, she knew it with a fatalistic certainty. Still she couldn't give up. It wasn't in her nature.

Desperately, Cassie jettisoned her sodden pack to prevent being sucked into the depths. If she were caught amongst the debris and weeds, she would drown. She tried again to swim but was unable to fight the current.

She was rapidly being swept into more turbulent and dangerous floodwaters, where this branch of the river merged with the main stream. She submerged and rose again, choking on water and mud. The bloated body of a kangaroo swept past and she shuddered with horror.

Obeying the instinctive need to survive, Cassie tried floating on her back; she was dragged under again and again by the pull of the current. Desperate for air, she fought to the surface, only to be overwhelmed by the force of the flow.

Terrified, Cassie felt the water close over her head once more, sucking her into the depths of the river. She knew she was failing, and battled with single-minded will, but in the end she wasn't strong enough.

Cassie's whole being screamed silently for Jack. She knew she should have heeded his advice, bitterly regretted not listening to him. She gritted her teeth trying not to cry out. Her lungs craved oxygen, she needed all her strength and concentration as she strove to reach the surface, her arms a heavy weight as they lost what little energy she had in reserve.

She needed Jack now as she had never needed him before, but to her sorrow she had left him, thinking she could manage on her own against all the forces of nature in this untamed land. What a fool she had been.

Suddenly Cassie felt a new pain in her head. Something caught her long hair, dragging her up to the surface. She felt arms supporting her exhausted body, towing her through the water until she was lying in the shallows on the bank of the flooded river.

After her stomach finished throwing up muddy water, she turned her head weakly, and saw Jack stretched out beside her, hanging on to a tree with one hand, her arm held tightly above the elbow with the other. He was breathing deeply, eyes closed as if in pain.

"Jack, thank God it's you. I thought I was finished." Cassie's voice rasped painfully as she gasped for air like a stranded fish, trying to stop trembling. She looked at him lying in the water. When he didn't reply, asked, "Jack. Are you okay?" She was overwhelmingly conscious of one thing, he had saved her life, again.

Suddenly he rose from the water dragging her up with him. "Of course I'm not okay," he shouted hoarsely. "I'm sick and tired of running after an irresponsible brat like you. I've just lost ten years of my life watching you being swept downstream to almost certain death. Of all the brainless, idiotic things to do, you seem to have topped them all." He seemed not to realize the punishing grip he had on her arm.

Cassie prized his fingers loose, shaking herself free, shouting back in an equally hoarse voice, "Don't yell at me." The fact that he'd been worried about her was something she would think about later.

She tried to take a step backwards, but her legs were like jelly, unable to support her. She stood still, putting her hand on a fallen tree branch for support. She was chilled to the bone, shaking with the reaction to her near drowning.

Shock made her nauseous, creating a metallic taste in her mouth. Jack turned and walked away a few paces, unable to stand still. He bowed his head as if in pain.

He turned to look back at her. "Suicide is what I'm talking about. I assume from your actions that you planned to drown yourself." Sarcasm dripped off Jack's tongue as he came to terms with the devastation he'd felt, confronted by her impending loss of life.

"How dare you take a chance like that? Isn't it enough that you ran away from me, did you have to throw your life away as well?" Jack was strong, but he felt himself weakening at the thought of what could have happened if he hadn't got to her in time.

Better to scare her into being sensible and have her hating him, rather than let her put her life at risk again.

Cassie was shaken at his words. She tried to hide her guilt with an angry response. It was as if she had lost control of her tongue. "Don't be an idiot, of course I wasn't trying to drown myself. I can swim perfectly well, probably better than you. I've got certificates."

"So have I." He didn't say what kind but continued, "You think you can swim better than me do you? I reckon I'll throw you back in the water. It's obviously what you'd prefer." He brushed his wet hair from his eyes, striding towards her, frustrated anger oozing out of every pulsating pore.

She turned and attempted to run, but he caught her easily, lifting her up in his arms. She fought and squirmed, pulling his hair, trying to overbalance him and escape. "Put me down you Neanderthal. I'm not someone you can push around. I'll get you for this!"

To a certain extent she achieved her object. He did overbalance, but he took her with him, turning so the full weight of his slender antagonist came down on him.

She instantly tried to push herself into an upright position with her hands on his chest. Cassie's feet slipped on the rocks, her lower body fitting itself to his as if it was made to be there. The water provided a cushion for their bodies, and Jack's arms closed firmly around her, preventing escape.

He refused to allow her to move away, pulling her down towards him, his senses attuned to her labored breathing, his flesh needing to join with hers, uncontrollably. She'd called him Neanderthal, and he knew that was what he was, a caveman with only one thing on his mind, claiming his woman. Possible procreation of the species never entered his head.

Without thinking of the consequences, he rolled over and anchored Cassie beneath him, touching his lips to hers, kissing her deeply and slowly, tasting her, encouraging her to taste him. It was something he had needed to do since he first set eyes on her on that dusty outback track. For a moment she struggled, then she gave in to the sensuous electricity he generated, moving her body in a timeless expression of need. It wasn't capitulation; it was an affirmation of life at it's most primitive.

Cassie felt as though she were being absorbed into his bloodstream, his heart beating in time with hers, creating frantic magnetism within them both. She had no idea how long they lay there in the water making the turbulence of the river seem tame by comparison with their emotions, but her senses knew the moment he started to change.

Heat that had been flowing to her from Jack's inner

life force was swiftly cut off leaving Cassie devastated with confusion and need. What the hell had gone wrong?

She could hardly breathe as she tried to find an answer inside herself. Somehow her throat had closed, preventing her speaking aloud. Not that it would have done any good to speak. She simply didn't know what to say.

Five

Jack rolled off Cassie and stood up, casting her adrift from him, both mentally and physically. He was breathing hard. Swiftly, he walked a few steps away, leaving her lying in the shallows of the river. A few moments later, she came to her senses and climbed to her feet, saying caustically, her voice not quite steady, "Well, now that we've got that out of the way, I suppose we can get out of here. I happen to be cold and wet."

Her inner fury was out of proportion to his crime of rejecting her but she could not help her reaction. It was like a physical pain in her heart, and she was fighting back with all she had.

Jack had been about to turn and reach out to her, but he held back, thinking, it's just as well. She had reminded him she was cold and wet. He should be thankful things hadn't gone too far. He noticed her shiver but didn't dare touch her. That would start the ball rolling again and be couldn't afford to let it happen. Not now. He ordered his recalcitrant body to fall into line. He just wasn't sure it was listening.

He said, his voice caustic too, "Just be grateful you can feel anything, Cassie. You could have been floating down the river instead of shooting your mouth off at me."

Cassie turned and grinned, reminding him of his sister, Ronnie, in a tormenting mood. "You think that's shooting my mouth off?" she taunted. "You should see me with my brothers. They've invested in a gag factory just to shut me up."

Jack tried not to laugh. She had broken all the rules of survival out here, and he meant to make sure trouble didn't find her again. He turned away before she could see his grin. "Just don't go off by yourself. It's too dangerous."

"All right Mr. Macho, you've made your point. It's obvious that I can't cross the river at this point. My pack seems to have gone as well." She looked around.

"What did you have in it?"

"My clothes, a few survival rations."

Jack frowned. "Did you think at all before you decided on such a hare-brained scheme?"

"I was only trying to reach a main road. I need to get out of here and I knew you wouldn't help me." Cassie put her hand up to probe the laceration on her temple.

"I couldn't help you, Cassie. I would have if I could. What's wrong with your head?"

"Nothing." She wasn't about to give him any more ammunition to use against her.

"Let me have a look," he insisted.

"I'm fine, Jack." He put his hand out to touch her and she recoiled from him. "Look, I said I'm okay." Every time this man got close to her, he raised her temperature, one way or another.

"All right you stubborn girl, have it your way. But don't expect me to carry you later on if you can't walk."

"There's no way I'd expect a man to carry me. Ever. I can get myself from one place to another without help from anyone."

"I'm sure you can, but don't forget, we're alone out here. I might need a hand sometimes as well."

"Of course I'd help, if I could." She grinned cheekily, suddenly revived at the prospect of him pleading for assistance. "I'm not sure I'm up to carrying a man with so much ...muscle."

Her eyes took in his large frame, lingering longest on his long strong legs and wide shoulders. Even though he was saturated with river water, Jack's ratty old clothes had no adverse effect on his masculinity. In fact they seemed to enhance his untamed appearance to the point where a girl would willingly live in a cave with him. Her throat went dry as she pictured him clad in nothing but a loincloth.

Jack looked at her suspiciously as she licked her lips. What had she been thinking? Nothing good he thought. She had that innocent look she'd reserved for moments of inspired wickedness. He said, "Let's get back to camp. At least there's food there, and a shelter of sorts. We might even find a towel or two."

They'd been walking for a few minutes when he took hold of Cassie's arm and stopped her, a scowl on his face. "Where are your boots?"

She was reluctant to tell him, knowing what he would say. "They're in the river."

He shook his head. "I don't know how you've survived up till now."

"I'll be fine. I have very tough feet."

"Tell me that again when we reach camp. If you aren't limping, I might believe you." He started walking again. Before long Cassie's feet were beginning to burn from contact with gritty, red sand and gravel. She didn't say a word.

As they walked through the hills, Cassie thought about that kiss at the water's edge. Was it only one? It was shattering to realize how little life had prepared her for that moment. She was twenty-three years old, and no one had ever before kissed her in a way that had made her forget her own name. She could still taste it, burning on her lips.

Her resolution to remain independent had faded. Suddenly she wanted to be a participant in life, not just an observer. She wondered what it would be like to have a relationship with a man who encouraged her to be true to her own ideals and respected her. She had been convinced that such a man did not exist outside the imagination, but now she found herself hoping that he did exist in reality.

She wondered why she should be thinking this way just because Jack had kissed her. I must be going crazy she thought. It's time to do the rounds of my friends before I'm tempted to register for the spinster club.

Jack was thinking much the same thing. He was worried that he was becoming too attracted to the wildcat he had brought to his previously peaceful camp. It was time to go home and rediscover his life. Surely he had some friends who weren't married.

There he was, thinking about marriage again. He realized he'd been thinking that word ever since he'd been turned inside out by carrot colored hair and a cheeky grin. He'd never done that in his life before, there seemed to be no escape from it.

The outback was really getting to him. He had to return to civilization as soon as possible, if not sooner. When they reached the camp Jack said, "Go inside the tent, Cassie. I'll find you something to wear until your clothes dry out."

"I'm not taking my clothes off while you sit outside. No way."

"Would you rather I came inside?" The look she gave him would fry the skin off a lizard. "Look, I'm not so desperate for a woman that I'd bother with a skinny red-head like you," he lied.

"There's no need to get personal. And I'm not skinny."

No, she wasn't skinny, thought Jack as he contemplated her slender curves. She was perfect. His hands itched to touch so he hurriedly busied himself hunting for a dry shirt.

"Come on, brat. I don't want to have to nurse you through pneumonia as well." Jack's voice was muffled as he rifled through his clothes. Nothing seemed anywhere near the right size for her.

"As well as what?" she snarled as she shivered.

Jack looked up, feeling justified. He held up his callused hand, one finger at a time. "One, I rescued you from being stranded on a desert track, where the only things alive were crows and lizards. Two, I saved you from being eaten alive by ants. Three, I saved you from starvation. I cooked. Four, I saved your life, twice if I recall. Once from a wild boar. Once from the river. Need I go on?"

"I suppose not," she conceded. "Don't let it go to your head though, it's a long way to the ground, and the bigger you are, the harder you fall." She hurried into the tent and hurriedly undressed, wrapping herself in a scratchy old blanket.

Outside, Jack muttered, "You have to have the last word, don't you, Cassie?" Then he grinned. He wouldn't have it any other way. When he found a tee shirt for her, he knew it would swim on her small frame; it was the best he could do.

Cassie hesitated before tossing her wet clothes out of the tent. She trusted him, most of the time, but she didn't entirely trust herself. She held out her hand, keeping the rest of her body out of sight. Jack passed her a pair of ratty old khaki pants that needed to be rolled up five times at the cuffs, and a piece of baling twine to hold them up. A black 'SAVE THE WHALES' tee shirt completed her outfit. "I haven't any boots to fit you," he told her when she emerged from the tent. "You'll have to go barefoot."

"Won't be the first time. Are you going to nag about my missing boots forever?"

"No point. It's a lost cause. Just remember. Look out for snakes."

"Thanks for the warning. At least I won't have to worry about shaking my boots before I put them on. The scorpions and centipedes will have free access to my feet."

Jack looked at her tiny, delicate feet, and grinned. "Such pretty feet too. It's tough."

Cassie held his spare pants up around her slim waist. As she tightened the baling twine in a knot she grimaced. "I could fit four of me in here, Jack."

He laughed. "Four Cassies. Now that would be scary. Grab your hat, girl. We're going fishing." When she looked mutinous, he said, "You're coming with me. That way I can keep an eye on you."

"Keep an eye on yourself," she muttered. He took a step towards her and she said, "all right, keep your shirt on, I'm coming."

"It's you who has to keep my shirt on."

"Just a technicality," she asserted. "This t-shirt looks like a dress on me?"

He was hard pressed not to laugh out loud as the whales cavorted every time she moved. "You look charming as usual, but perhaps I better give you another piece of twine to tie your hair back, otherwise we won't catch any fish."

"Oh, why is that?" she asked.

"They'd take one look at your red hair and run for cover."

"You're a dinosaur, Jack. An uncivilized beast with a very primitive sense of humor. It's going to get you into trouble one of these days."

"I think I'm already in trouble," he replied enigmatically, and led the way down to the river where they spent the rest of the day fishing.

Two days later, Jack took his rifle and went hunting. Cassie promised him when he left, she'd stay near the camp. The floodwaters had gone down considerably leaving large expanses of mud and tangled vegetation at the water's edge. She had caught glimpses of wild horses but, as soon as they were close enough to sense her presence, they galloped away, leaving the river edge trampled.

The vantage point on the hill was where Cassie chose to sit, watching the river as it flowed through the water hole and out again. She did this at every opportunity, managing to see, not only horses, but dingoes, parrots, cockatoos, galahs, kangaroos and other wildlife as well, even a few wild pigs. She even saw a flock of tiny green budgerigars fly overhead, envying their freedom of flight.

The previous day Cassie had looked through Jack's plant diary. It wasn't exactly her choice of reading material, but she was bored sitting around all day, waiting for the flood to go down.

Before he left to go hunting that morning, Jack had told her they'd soon be able to walk to another campsite he frequented. From there it was not far to Jasper Creek. He suggested, in the meantime, that they check out the river area for semi-precious stones and fossils. Cassie was glad to have something positive to do at last.

As soon as he'd gone, she collected a hessian bag from the shelter, setting off down the slippery hill. She knew just where to place her feet as she had taken several spills on her way to and from the water. Out of necessity she had worked out a way to avoid disaster.

Clumps of grass, small tough bushes and a few large boulders off the path provided handy anchoring points, preventing an ignominious slide into the river. The path twisted and turned past stubby trees, leafy branches preventing her seeing around the next corner. Several large trees also provided shade for a stop on the way.

When Cassie reached the river, she set off to where a shallow creek connected to the main flow. Not having been inundated with mud from the flood, the water in the creek flowed clearly over rocks that lined the creek bed. It was an ideal place to look for gemstones. Even if she didn't find anything, she knew it would be hard to find a more idyllic spot to while away the time. It was so peaceful just sitting in the shade of a eucalyptus tree, watching the birds, dreaming of Jack.

"So this is where you got to!" Jack said as he came up behind Cassie. "You should have told me where you were going. You've been gone hours."

"Jack!" Cassie jumped up, startled. She hadn't expected him to follow her. "Is something wrong? Why are you back so soon?"

"What's the matter, did I interrupt you while you were doing something important?"

"There's no need to be like that. I'm only having a break from gem hunting."

He paced up and down, kicking sand as he went. "I suppose it didn't occur to you that I might be concerned for your safety?" He refused to admit, even to himself, he had missed her company.

"No, not really. After all, you told me about this place."

"You were supposed to wait until I came back to camp, Cassie."

"Oh, was I? I don't remember you being appointed my guardian."

"I was only thinking of you."

"I don't think so, Jack. You just love telling people what to do."

"I'm only telling you because you need to be told. Women do things differently than men. I reckon hormones have something to do with it."

While Cassie digested this piece of logic, an idea came to her. "Do you mean to suggest that females react differently to men in any situation? Because of hormones."

Jack should have been alerted by the sweet reasonable tones of Cassie's voice.

He said, "I certainly do. Women are at the mercy of their hormones, and their emotions. When offered a choice of something they always go by how they feel, their emotions, not by whether it's right or good or whether they need whatever it is."

Warming to his subject, he missed the gleam of triumph in his opponent's eye. "Take shopping for instance. If I decide to buy a pair of shoes, I always work out first what I want to use them for. Then I look at what's available and make my choice, logically, taking everything into account. A woman, however, will buy shoes and without considering first where she wants to wear them.

"She'll look around the store, trying on every shoe in sight, if she likes the look of them. She gives no thought to durability or practicality, only whether she likes the style or color. Now tell me Cassie, is that a logical way to behave?"

"Perfectly logical. Whether you agree or not, style and color are important. But you stated women are ruled by emotions. Don't you think men are too?"

"No. Men are straightforward, none of this mucking around with nerves and emotions. We leave that to you women." It was amazing how vocal he became when he wanted to put his point across. Cassie was most impressed.

She had been steadily edging closer to Jack as he talked, and paced. He looked startled as she put her small hand on his sleeve. "Jack," she said softly, "I believe you said something about wanting to come down to the river with me. I'm glad you're here now because I'd like you to carry some of these stones back to camp for me. I'd like to take a closer look at them but there's too many for me to take all at once."

He looked down at her and grinned, "Sure. I can do that. Where are they?"

"Over there." Cassie pointed to where the hessian bag lay near the tree. "Wait until I wash these rocks here, then I'll have all the ones I need for now."

"Let me help." He scooped up her booty and strode over to the water. As he passed Cassie, she turned, as if by accident, causing him to bump into her.

He dropped the rocks, reaching out to steady her as she fell forward into his arms, stepping on his foot in the process.

"Oh dear," she said breathlessly. "I'm sorry Jack. I'm so clumsy. Did I hurt you?"

"How could you hurt me? I've got boots on, your feet are bare." He looked down into her face and swallowed. "Your legs are bare as well."

"I know." Her eyes never left his face. "Yours are too." She could feel the muscles of his thighs flexing as he moved, rubbing on her smooth, slender legs. She moved a little to steady herself, creating a dangerous friction between them. "I can feel them."

"So can I." He didn't move away. He couldn't.

She caressed his shoulders, standing close to him in the shade of the tree, enveloped by his strength, his indomitable masculinity. "You're so strong Jack, so big. I feel as if I can trust you with anything, even my life." Moistening her parched lips with her tongue, she became a victim of her own conspiracy. She whispered, "Jack, would you do something for me? Please."

"Anything. Name it," he choked out roughly, trying to breathe.

"Would you kiss me? A friendly kiss. Nothing more. I need to know I'm not a burden to you, that you like me just a little. If you kiss me, I'll know."

"I think I could manage that," said Jack huskily, not intending the kiss to be more than a swift touch of the lips, a balm to her fragile feminine nerves. He had no intention of letting her know how he felt, how much he wanted to push her down on the sand and make love to her until they were both exhausted and satisfied.

The moment his lips touched hers he knew he had made a fatal error in judgment. The light pressure he exerted was instantly returned tenfold. Like metal to a magnet, her lips moved in a dance of desire all the more exciting for its untrained nature.

She seemed capable of extracting every last ounce of emotion he possessed. He was unable to remain aloof in such a heated embrace. Rational thought was suspended as he was compelled to feed the flames that licked at him into a raging inferno. His body knew what it wanted as it responded with feverish pleasure, urged on by the fervent yet unskilled seduction of the girl in his arms.

Jack knew, logically, that a man couldn't die from unfulfilled desires, but that didn't prevent him experiencing agonizing mental and physical pain as he wrenched himself away from her. He could not, and would not, violate the trust she had placed in him, even at the cost of his sanity and health. "We have to stop this," he gasped, holding her at arms length when she would have returned to him.

Cassie was burning. What had started out as a tease to get Jack to admit to his emotions had rapidly escalated into a passionate explosion of need on her part and, she could tell, on his as well? On reflection, when she took a calming breath, she could see he was right. It would be disastrous for them to continue this any further.

He was not a man she should become involved with. Pride was stung however, that he could once again reject her so easily. Her voice was cutting as she retorted, "I believe you said something about hormones dictating the way women react? Do you expect me to believe that only my hormones were involved just now? What about yours, hmm? Doesn't testosterone count?"

Jack reddened under his tan. "Trust a woman to remember every little detail."

"I know what I felt, Jack. I remember it all. Everything you said,"sShe paused, allowing her gaze to wander, "and everything you did."

Suspicion suddenly raised its head. Jack glared at Cassie, who waited. "Did you, by any chance, pull that little stunt on purpose?"

"What little stunt?" she asked, her innocence flawed.

He glared at her. "Cassie," he warned.

"Oh, all right," she grumbled. "I wanted to remind you that you're human. Men have emotions too, you know, it's not a crime to show them now and then."

"I think you need to be reminded just how dangerous it is to stir guys up without intending to follow through." Jack pulled his boots and socks off. As he walked towards her, she turned and ran. Before she had gone more than a few steps, he scooped her up in a fireman's lift, carrying her over his shoulder to a muddy puddle.

She shrieked, slapping his firm backside. "Put me down, you barbarian."

"Okay." Wading into the mud up to his knees, he suddenly let her go. She clung to his neck, trailing her feet in the brown mud, kicking, and trying to keep from falling in.

"Please, Jack," she cried, half laughing now, trying to lift her feet clear. "Take me back to dry land. I'll be good from now on. I won't stir you up any more. I promise."

"He looked down at her solemnly as he put her back on the bank. "You better not, Cassie, because next time I might not be able to stop."

"What won't you be able to stop, Jack?" She couldn't resist one more tease.

"All right, Cassie, since you insist. I wouldn't be able to stop making love to you."

"What if I want it too? I'm old enough to make my own decisions."

"It doesn't make any difference. I have to protect you, even if you don't want me to. If you tease me any more I'll have to cool you off in the river. Come on, I'll see you back to camp, and then we'll have lunch. I need to go hunting. We've still got to eat."

"Why did you come back?"

"I forgot my knife. When I came back, you were gone. Don't ever do that again, Cassie. I'm likely to be a nervous wreck if you keep disappearing like that."

"I promise, Jack. I'll leave a note from now on, okay."

"You better. Otherwise I might do something we'll both regret."

Cassie didn't reply, just turned away towards the camp, thinking, maybe he'd regret it, but I'm not sure I would. It might just be worth it to feel his arms around me once more.

Six

The sun was going down in a blaze of glory, the sky taking on every hue of the rainbow, tinting clouds green, blue and vivid orange. Brown and gray shadows blended with magenta, alizarin crimson and mauve. As the clouds moved on, shadows faded to tan and beige, becoming a misty pale gray.

The air was cool as Cassie waited for Jack to return from hunting. Hearing the thud of firm shod hooves in the sodden terrain and a faint snorting exhale, her curiosity was piqued at the obvious sound of horses. Excited at the prospect of catching her first glimpse of brumbies, the wild horses inhabiting the open plains of the outback, she hurried to her favorite lookout and lay on her stomach, listening, watching. Scanning the view, she couldn't see anything, just the usual milieu of terracotta earth rising to meet a vast sapphire sky. She leaned forward, eyes straining, thinking that she must have imagined hearing them. The land spread out before her, mysterious in the shadows.

As she waited she heard a man's voice behind her. "Get a load of this, Blue."

"Wow, Kev. It's female," said Blue. "Wonder what she's doin' here?"

"Dunno, mate. Why don't you ask her?" Kev sniggered.

"Why don't you?" Blue gave Kev a poke in the ribs with the butt of his rifle.

"Yeah, mate, I reckon I will," Kev said as he moved

out of Blue's way. "But I get first go, okay? Can't let a bastard like you have all the fun."

When Cassie heard this exchange, her blood chilled. She immediately jumped to her feet, backing away from the rocks where the voices originated. She watched warily as two men entered the clearing. They had rifles in their hands.

The men looked rough. She remembered belatedly that Jack had told her to disappear fast if the people he was expecting turned up. Now she was trapped.

She stood still, poised for flight. "Who are you?"

The two men looked at each other, then back at Cassie, eyes greedy, reflecting their elation at finding a woman alone. They laughed.

The red haired man said, "I'm Blue. We were looking for Jack. We found you instead. What a surprise. Our luck's turned around."

Cassie's mouth went dry as the dark man's eyes roved over her like tiny black slugs.

"Don't listen to him, darlin'. I'm Kev. What's your name pretty lady?"

She found her voice. "None of your business."

Kev said, "Now, don't be like that. I haven't had a woman in a month of Sundays, so I'm about ready for some R and R?"

Cassie moved backwards, knowing she was in serious trouble. Hoping for a reprieve, she looked behind the two men. She said, "Jack is on his way back right now. He told me he was expecting someone."

The two men looked around and laughed. Kev said, "So why isn't he here?"

"I told you. He's on his way."

"He's not here now, Kev." Blue licked his lips. "We've got time."

Cassie shrank back, trying to think what she could do. Her mind was a blank.

Kev casually dragged a packet of cigarettes from under his rolled up sleeve, watching her with rapacious eyes. He said, "I think we'll take her with us, Blue. More fun for later on. We don't want to be interrupted."

Blue reached over and took one of Kev's cigarettes. "Sounds good, Kev. I'm in." His eyes moved restlessly over Cassie. She shivered with disgust. Her reaction brought a smile of anticipation to his dissipated face.

Wearing a greasy felt hat with a dirty blue plaid shirt, Blue had squeezed into a pair of disreputable jeans, holes in the knees and the seat. She could smell him coming closer. Describing him as rancid was overstating his appeal. Under his beefy arm, his rifle was pointed to the ground, but it gave him power.

Cassie stuck her chin out belligerently. "Get away from me." She refused to let them see her fear, which was pulsating in a steady throb beneath her breast.

"Now don't get nasty, darlin'. We're just blokes who want a bit of fun. Nothin' wrong with that." Kev seemed marginally less frightening to Cassie, but she knew he was still dangerous. "You wouldn't want us to feel unwelcome would you?" He turned, looking out over the water as Cassie had done. He seemed to be searching for something.

"If you know what's good for you, you'll disappear," she said, edging toward the path that led down to the water.

"Yeah, but you're coming' with us. We'll come back to see Jack tomorrow." His grin was evil. "Or the next day. In the meantime we'll have ourselves a party."

"He'll come looking for me."

"No, he won't." Kev spat a stream of dirty fluid onto

the ground at her feet. "He'll think you've gone swimming, or something. You'll leave him a note. By the time he realizes you aren't coming back, it'll be too late to go looking. When we turn up tomorrow, we'll kindly help him search for you. Too bad we won't find you." He tossed his cigarette down, adding, "It's been a dry year."

Blue laughed. "Yeah, he spent it behind bars, playing toy boy."

Kev glanced at Blue with hard eyes. "We're going to have a little talk, Blue, old son. When we've finished with Jack, I'll show you some tricks I learned in the can."

Blue gulped. "I didn't mean…" his voice trailed off."

Kev said, "Yeah, you did. And you'll pay." Then he reached for Cassie's arm.

She shook him off and backed away. "I'm not going anywhere with you two idiots."

Kev looked her up and down, his face burned almost black from the sun, his teeth in urgent need of repair. "Jack might get hassled if we steal his woman. Better he thinks you took off on your own. Less bloodshed." She went white. He grinned. "Don't worry, darlin', I won't hurt you much, if you're nice to me. But first, I want to know what you're doin' out here with Jack? Are you in the drug business too?"

"What! Drugs? No, I've got better things to do with my time." Was this what Jack was involved in? Drugs. She could hardly believe it.

"What things?" Kev was breathing in her face, making her feel sick.

"None of your business," she snapped, repelled by the unwashed odor emanating from the two men. Blue had been slowly edging closer, making her want to throw up.

"So, where'd Jack disappear to?" Kev glanced around

as if Jack might suddenly appear out of thin air. "I want to make sure we don't run into him on the way."

"He only went to get water, so he'll be back any minute. I told you that."

"Yeah, but which direction?" Kev scratched his stubbled jaw, narrowing his eyes as Cassie backed further away. He followed, his hot gaze on his prey, not realizing they were coming to the edge of the clearing where the hidden path leading down to the water began. His scrawny frame loomed over Cassie menacingly.

She tried to remember the defensive moves her brothers had taught her, none came immediately to mind. They'd been skilled at fending her off, and she'd had no one else to practice on. The added danger was that these predators had rifles. She might survive rape, but bullets were another story.

Blue had now prowled close enough to stroke Cassie's hair. He reached out, his hands encrusted with dirt. She jumped back. "If you lay one finger on me, I'll make you wish Jack had found you first."

Blue laughed, the sound humorless and grating. "That's a good one. Hey Kev, we've got ourselves a funny girl. I think I'm gonna enjoy having her along for the ride."

"Yeah." Kev grinned as his gaze strolled over Cassie's defensive figure. "She looks like she'll fight back. Should be a fun night."

Cassie desperately wished Jack would turn up. It was unlikely that he would hear her scream for help, and she knew it, so she decided it was now or never. Elbowing Blue in the stomach, she took off down the hill, zigzagging through the scrub on her own previously used pathway.

Kev tried to grab her, but fell on his face in the dirt. He was up again in a second, spitting out sand and gravel, still too late to stop her escape. "Come on, Blue," he shouted. "Not gonna let a woman beat ya, hey?" He took off at a run, heading down through the bushes where his quarry had disappeared.

"No way, mate," Blue agreed, breathlessly holding his stomach. "I reckon she needs a lesson in manners. Let's cut her off." Then he gave a scream of rage and fright as he slipped and fell onto his well-padded backside, his rifle discharging in the process.

A mudslide had formed on the hillside. In seconds he was hurtling full throttle down a slippery slope, unable to stop or slow down, taking Kev along for the ride. The two men landed in the river at the bottom of the slope, bruised and bleeding, taking a bath for the first time in weeks. Their rifles sank into the muddy water.

Crawling out of the river a few minutes later, like primeval slime, Kev and Blue shook their heads, spitting out muddy water. Kev's voice was hoarse from yelling. He looked at Blue and croaked, "Reckon she done us in, mate. We'll have to get her for that, the bitch. Where's your gun? I dropped mine in the river."

"Me too." Blue breathed hard, gasping like an asthmatic. "We'll have to get even, that's for bloody sure. I owe her a punch in the guts for starters."

They pulled up short at the sight of the tall man standing on the bank nearby. He was regarding them with a black scowl. If they thought he looked angry enough to carve his name into their hides, they were right.

On his way back to camp with fresh water from a spring, he had seen and heard enough to know they planned to kidnap Cassie. He'd expected Blue and Kev to turn up some time soon, but he hadn't foreseen this. When he'd heard the rifle go off, he felt like he'd been kicked in the stomach, fear curling like a snake inside him, ready to strike.

"You guys having a good time?" he asked, his polite tone a warning. He'd had a few minutes to contain his rage but it was still there, waiting like a crouching beast, ready to rip them limb from limb.

Kev and Blue looked at Jack, then at each other, wordlessly communicating their desire to be gone. He might be a research scientist, but he was a dangerous man. Anyone who said no to Gerald Silverton, and got away with it, had guts. Jack had said no to Silverton's demands to control his drug research, and survived.

Cassie stood a little way up the slope, breathing hard. She said nothing, just watching Kev and Blue. They were a pathetic pair of ruffians, mangy wet dogs shivering and dripping in the breeze. Then she looked into Kev's eyes and saw the cornered predator watching her, and shivered. What would he do when his only way out was to fight? She already knew the answer. He would attack anyone who stood in his way.

"Hey, Jack," said Kev, his eyes shifting. "What are you doin' here?"

Blue stood, silently bovine, waiting for Kev to retrieve the situation, his feet squelching in soggy boots. This sucks, he thought. He caught Cassie watching him and glared. She could see he remembered her elbow in his stomach, and moved back slightly. He might be round, short and hairy, but he was no cuddly teddy bear.

"I was looking for you two guys." Jack's expression was benign, but somehow an underlying danger was clear. Even Cassie felt its power as she watched the men. Something primitive seemed to be waiting to break loose. She would have welcomed it if she hadn't had that brief glimpse into what was left of Kev's soul. There was an emptiness, a lack of humanity, that told of a depth of depravity that was waiting to be tapped. This was good versus evil at it's most elemental.

Then, Kev tried to grin. He misfired, snarling instead. Cassie was left feeling that something repulsive had crawled over her skin. She rubbed her hands on her shirt, but the slug trail remained. He said, "Lighten up, Jack. We're here to do business, aren't we? You know Mr. Silverton needs that research map. He offered a fair price."

"And I said no deal. End of story." Jack moved his rifle from hand to hand but didn't take his eyes off Kev.

Blue licked his lips nervously. "We came looking for you, Jack." His eyes were calculating his chances, shifting from Jack to Cassie. "Guess we found you, hey?"

"Guess you did. What are you doing in the water?" Jack flexed his hands as he waited.

Blue looked at Cassie with venom. "She attacked me."

"What did you do to her?"

Blue said, "Nothin'. She just pushed me down the hill for no reason. I hit rocks on the way down. Fall could've killed me."

"Pity it didn't." Jack watched Kev's hands. He knew Kev kept a knife strapped to his ankle, and was ready in case the man made a move. "Guess I'll have to do it myself."

Kev didn't seem to hear Jack's comment. He was wiping the water and mud from his stringy black hair, streaking slime down to his chin. All Cassie could think of was slug trails. Blue plucked his shirt away from his stomach, making a sucking sound to match his boots. His jeans were sagging so much they were falling off. Not a pretty sight.

Jack said, "I watched you come down the hill, sliding

in the mud. Looked like you couldn't wait to get down here. Needed a bath did you?" he mocked, knowing it would provoke a reaction. They really were a sorry sight but he didn't make the mistake of taking his eyes off them. Kev had a reputation for viciousness, gained while serving a prison term for theft and assault with a deadly weapon. His skill with a knife was well known in the Territory, learned when he worked at an abattoir in Darwin.

Earlier, Jack had seen Cassie coming as fast as she could towards the bottom of the hill, trying to keep a foothold with bare feet on the slippery clumps of grass. His heart had been in his throat all the way. Somehow he had felt her fear as well. Then he'd heard the gunshot, and his life had changed.

Kev and Blue were like rats in a trap. They would bite the hand that fed them right up to the elbow if he underestimated them. Silverton owned them, and he used them for his own purposes. They had no morality, no sense of honor. All they wanted, they took, without looking back at the carnage they left behind. If they had been born with any redeeming features, they had been washed away in booze and drugs throughout many years of self-indulgence.

"Get out of the way, Jack. We've had enough of this crap." Kev began to walk toward the path back up the hill, but stopped as Jack moved forward, his eyes watchful.

"Got a party to go to?" Jack asked, still polite. "I insist you finish your bath. Can't have you turning up at Jasper Creek pub smelling like bums."

He called over his shoulder. "Cassie, get some soap will you? There's some in my pack. I need to figure out what to do with these two scum-bags, but I can't stand the stink while I do it."

"Call the police," she said.

"Can't. No phone. Remember?"

"Yeah. What a pain." Then she grinned. Jack had the upper hand. There was nothing to worry about now. "I'll get the soap and leave you to think about it. Be right back," then she started up the hill, nimbly bypassing the mudslide.

There was tense silence for a moment, the air vibrating with leashed hostility.

Jack said, "You two got another line of work you can do? Besides whacking people for Gerald Silverton, that is?"

Kev glared at him. "Silverton pays well. What's it to you, anyway?"

"When you go back without the map, your jobs are history. So are you."

"You've got the map here haven't you?" Blue looked worried.

"Yeah, but I did some more research into Silverton and his business. I don't like his reputation so I've decided to keep the map, and all the other research."

"You can't do that," said Kev. "You'll be cutting your own throat. No-one's that stupid."

"You are. You work for Silverton. He grows and sells drugs. In case you didn't realize, that's illegal. You also did yourselves in the moment you attacked my woman."

Cassie liked the sound of that. Jack's woman. She had come back down the path with the soap and was listening to their exchange.

"Gotta make money, Jack. Got debts." Blue looked jittery. "Man's gotta eat."

Kev snarled, "You need to starve. Shut up, Blue. I'll handle this."

Blue glared at Kev. "I lost poker money to Silverton. He's squeezing me dry."

"Yeah. I know. He'll break your legs if you don't pay." Kev laughed. "So what?"

"He's an animal," said Blue, bitterly. "He had to be cheating to win so much. Maybe if I could find another game. I could win enough to get back on my feet."

"Forget it," mocked Kev. "You're a loser, Blue."

"You're both losers." Jack had the measure of Blue's basic nature. There was a man who knew the importance of bootlicking and excelled at it. He had chewed brown leather many times in his life and clearly he hated the taste and texture of it. But still, he knew its value. He knew how to milk an opportunity to the full. It was too bad he'd just run out of chances.

Money was something that pulled strings with Kevin O'Shannassy. Money and power were the only things he respected, Jack was the possessor of both. Envy rode him constantly. The bitter pill was that his father had had money, and lost it gambling. Suicide had been his only option, leaving his family on welfare. Drugs were one way out for Kev, and he went down that road without looking back.

"You two better clean yourselves up. I can't help you with your drug running boss. He's an even bigger loser than you are." Jack turned away from the two men. Any understanding he might have felt for their wasted lives was wiped away by the memory of a gunshot. Cassie's safety was his priority. "When you get back to Alice Springs, tell Silverton I declined his offer. Again."

"He'll blame us," whined Blue.

Kev's face had taken on a hard, dark cast. He said, "He won't like it, Jack."

Jack nodded. "You could be right. Go somewhere else. How about South America?"

"Wherever we go, he'll find us." Kev looked into the distance, his future bleak by anyone's estimation.

Cassie almost felt sorry for him until she remembered what they had planned for her.

Kev turned to Jack and laughed, the sound chilling. "He won't blame us, Jack. He'll blame you. I'll make sure of it. I've already worked out what to say."

Cassie saw the darkness in Kev find a way to survive and knew he would destroy Jack in the process. She started to speak, but Jack looked at her and shook his head. She saw that he was aware of Kev's intent. It seemed he had a plan of his own.

"Silverton won't care who screwed up. He just wants the map, and the research. When he wants to talk, he'll contact me. We'll make a new deal, and you'll be history."

"Is this what I heard you talking about before, Jack? What kind of research? What map?" Cassie came up close behind him.

Kev laughed. "Yeah, tell her, Jack. Tell her how you planned to sell information to a drug dealer, for cold, hard cash."

"Is it true?"

"Sort of." Jack decided the truth was his best option. He didn't look at her as he explained. He was still watching Blue and Kev. They had the look of feral desperate men. "I do pharmaceutical research on rare plants to find medical uses for them. I discovered a hybrid poppy that thrives in a hot dry climate. It can be used to make a new variety of heroin. Unfortunately, it's still addictive, and it's perfect for use in designer drugs. One of the chemists in my company sold us out. Silverton found out about it and offered me a large amount of cash for the research and a map of where the plant can be found. The map is what these two are here to collect."

"I can't believe you'd do something like that, Jack?" She looked totally disillusioned.

"I was going to." Jack nearly choked on the lie. He couldn't tell her any more with Kev and Blue listening. They had to believe he would eventually go through with the deal. A lot depended on Silverton believing he had Jack in the palm of his hand. That all he had to do was offer the right incentive, and Jack would be his.

Jack glanced at Cassie from the corner of his eye. She was looking at him as if he were pond scum. Then she turned and walked away. He couldn't even watch her go because he had to keep his eye on Blue and Kev.

Kev said, "How about we make ourselves a new deal, Jack. We'll cut out Silverton altogether. I've got plenty of contacts that would pay for that information."

Jack laughed. "What do you think? That I'll forgive and forget when you tried to molest and kidnap a friend of mine. You really are a pair of idiots."

Blue disagreed. "We're not idiots. We didn't know she was a friend of yours. She could have been a tourist. No-one would have ever known."

"The police would. There'd be a statewide search when she didn't turn up. She's American so the FBI would come looking for you. People have friends, Blue. You don't, but you don't deserve any. You hustle at poker just as much as Silverton does. Even Kev wouldn't miss you"

Kev snorted. ""Are you kidding? Miss Blue? No way. He eats too much."

"And you're a scrawny pack rat," snarled Blue. "I saw them opals you pinched from that prospector on the road to Mt. Isa. You didn't even share them with me. I was the one who found him."

"And I was the one who fixed him, so shut up." Kev

turned to Jack. "Come on, Jack. Give us a break. We didn't do the woman. We even didn't know she was yours."

"Makes no difference. Tell me about the prospector." Jack's tone was hard.

"What are you, a boy scout?"

Jack glared at Kev who dismissed him with a shrug. "It was no big deal. We left him alive."

Blue said, "What was he gonna do with a pocket full of opals anyway? He'd just drink any money he got. Kev's got a wife back in Darwin. I need to buy a car so we need cash."

"Kev's wife probably hates him like everyone else," said Jack. "You could go back to your other job, Blue, stealing cars is very lucrative, I hear. Now cut the crap. Where and when did you leave the guy? If he's alive, he probably needs a doctor."

"He's back at Altuna Station. We left him by the side of the road yesterday. Someone would have found him. It's not our fault he couldn't walk. We gave him a stick."

"You are such a gentleman, Kev. He's probably singing your praises to the police right now." Jack shook his head in disgust. He knew he wouldn't get anything more out of them.

Jack said, "That's it. Get in the water you two mongrels. I need to work out what I'm going to do, and I can't think while you're standing there mouthing off." He lifted the rifle to show he was still in control. Blue stooped, and pulled off his boots. Kev didn't move for a long moment, and then he shrugged, and unbuttoned his shirt.

"Better take that knife off your ankle, Kev," said Jack. "You won't need it in the water. It'll get rusty. If you ever get another job at an abattoir, you'll need it."

"Bastard," Kev muttered, slowly unstrapping his knife sheath, laying it on the ground. Jack quickly kicked it out of the way. It was a dangerous weapon, a boning knife, capable of inflicting major damage. Kev kept it very sharp; it was the only work he took any pride in. He clearly wanted to make a lunge for it but after a moment of hesitation he gave up.

Kev snarled, "I won't forget this."

Jack grinned, saying, "Neither will I."

Jack could almost hear Kev's teeth grinding together as he wove fantasies of revenge. Stripping fast, the two men went into the cold river, soaping their pale naked bodies, washing hair that was stiff with dirt and mud. When they were finished, they stood waist deep in the river and shivered.

"Better wash these too." Jack kicked their clothes off the bank into the water.

While they washed their clothes, snarling at Jack and getting in each other's way, Blue and Kev were concentrating on staying upright in the water. The river was flowing well that day. Mosquitoes were also making inroads into bare flesh. Jack silently disappeared up the hill, leaving the men to their ablutions.

Once out of sight, Jack raced to the campsite, desperately hoping that Cassie would still be there.

She was, she had nowhere else to go.

With undisguised relief, he beckoned to her and whispered, "I think it's time we left. They might resurrect their rifles from the water. I don't know whether they'd work or not but I can't take that chance. We don't want a gunfight."

"Where will we go?" she asked.

"I know a place. We'll take their horses. It's better than walking and they won't be able to follow."

"Sounds good. Better hurry though. Can you hear them yelling about what they'll do when they catch us? I don't want to be made into hamburger at a dog food factory."

"Neither do I." Jack quickly grabbed his pack. They were ready to go. As they mounted, they could hear the two men coming up the hill, slipping and sliding, cursing anyone and everything as they climbed naked through the mud, dragging their wet clothes and boots behind them. They didn't know there was another way to go, and Cassie wasn't going to tell them. They'd have to sink or swim on their own.

As she urged her horse forward, Cassie set her jaw and looked into Jack's eyes. "Once we're safe from these crooks, you're on your own. I have no wish to be involved with a criminal."

Jack searched her face for any hint of the warmth he'd seen earlier, but this only proved to harden her resolve. "I'm not a criminal Cassie, you'll just have to trust me on this one." He nudged his horse into action, "Follow me, I promise, it will be okay." He repeated emphatically, "Please, just trust me."

Seven

THE solitude implied by the vastness of the landscape allowed them both to be alone with their thoughts on the long journey. Cassie was besieged by doubts and recriminations. How could she have allowed herself to be drawn in by Jack's deception? And, even worse, how could she have been so misguided in her feelings for him? He was nothing but a … a …miscreant! No wonder he looked so primitive, he was no better than the cavemen they had just left behind.

As if sensing her thoughts, Jack leaned towards her and said quietly, "It's not what you think. I wouldn't sell my drug research, Cassie. Not for any amount of money. I couldn't tell you that in front of our audience. They have to believe I'm as dirty as they are. We'll talk later, okay?"

She looked him straight in the eye. "Okay. But this better be on the up and up. I don't want any more surprises. If you're lying to me, I'll know. And then I'll be gone."

"It's a deal."

"I'd rather you didn't use that word, Jack."

"I never will again, I swear."

Jack was unable to sleep that night. After riding for hours, they had camped on a flat plain, surrounded by rocky outcrops and paper bark trees. The wild flowers after the rain were abundant, green grass was coming alive. They had no tent, just sleeping bags. In this northern fringe of the Simpson Desert, it was hard to find a piece of ground not covered with stones or coarse red sand. Their fire was their only source of light, apart from the moon.

Jack had said they would talk later about his involvement with drugs. Cassie decided now was a good time. "So, Jack, how come you told Silverton you'd sell him the information about your hybrid poppy? You know he'll use it to make drugs."

"I know. I initially refused, and he said he'd contact me again in case I changed my mind. He sounded quite civilized on the phone. The police have been watching him. I think they tapped his phone, that's how they knew about me. He's been making a name for himself, and they want to get him out of action before he does serious damage.

"Did he contact you again?"

"Yeah. He did. The police came to see me at my office in Melbourne." At Cassie's surprised look, he said, "I don't stay out here all the time. I have people working on this development for me. It's my company. This just happens to be my pet project, so, in light of the interest from Silverton, I took some time to work on it personally."

"You don't look like a business man."

"You don't look like a paleontologist," he returned. "Besides, when I put on a suit, I want people to know I mean business. Nothing gets done without my authority."

"What about your research chemist who sold you out to Silverton?"

"He'll be dealt with."

Jack sounded ruthless. Somehow she knew the suit he wore at his office couldn't hide the elemental power of his personality. He would be in total control. Blue and Kev were lucky. But for the lack of an effective communication network, they would have been cooling their heels in a cell at Alice Springs jail. Jack would have made sure of it.

"So what happened when the police came to see you?" Cassie wanted to know.

"They said he'd call again. They'd record the phone conversation. I was to accept his offer. They'd be on hand when someone turned up to collect.

"Where will that happen?"

"I have a small research laboratory, in the direction we're heading. I've been experimenting with the plants in their natural environment."

"He wouldn't come up here alone would he?"

"Probably not. He doesn't trust anyone, so he sets deals up himself, initially. After that he could send someone to collect the research results, and the map."

"Someone like Blue and Kev?"

"Yeah. Not them though. Someone with brains and fire-power."

"He's very organized isn't he?"

"Seems to be. I've never met the man in person. Police showed me photographs. When he contacted me the second time, I told him I was willing to renegotiate the deal, for a price. He thinks I'm like him, out for what I can get. Money. The police want to put him out of business but it seems I'm the only way they can do it."

"Yes, I see that. Are you sure you know what you're getting in to?

"No. But you've seen what kind of men Blue and Kev are. I was supposed to give them a diagram of the general area the plant was to be found. I drew it badly, but that's neither here nor there. It was a gesture of good faith on my part to Silverton. The police called it a teaser so he'd come up here himself to collect the map. Blue and Kev couldn't keep their mind on the job, hence that fiasco at Kalangadoo."

"They were a pair of animals, Jack."

"Yeah. But Silverton is ten times worse, only he hides it well. He's a businessman, but it's just a front for all his other enterprises. And he's sneaky. Plenty of offshore accounts to hide his drug money. The police told me he launders some of it through a bus tour business."

"When is this exchange of information supposed to take place?"

"The plant will be mature very soon. Silverton wants to see it growing. One of his men is a research chemist. He wants samples he can run tests on."

"So where is Silverton now?" Cassie looked around nervously, as if the man was too close for comfort. The only sound to be heard was an owl, another kind of predator.

"Probably back in Alice Springs. He runs the bus tour company himself, as a blind."

"Pity he didn't stick to that."

"Doesn't make enough money. Not for him."

"I'm glad you refused to sell the drug information to him, Jack."

Cassie smiled at him, making him feel as if it had all been worth it. They settled down on opposite sides of their campfire, talking, both on the edge of sleep.

Just as the sun rose the next day, Jack and Cassie climbed on the horses and headed for Jack's field camp. He'd been heading that way when he and had Cassie first met, taking some time off, hiking and looking for another rare plant he had heard of. It was also a time for him to think about the problem with Gerald Silverton, and how he was going to handle the exchange of information. Pressure was building, and he wanted to be prepared.

Now he was on his way again, only under much different circumstances. Cassie was with him, and she was a distraction. As they rode, his mind lingered over Cassie's slim curves and soft mouth. These days he was feeling very primitive indeed, not the dedicated businessman he had claimed to be. He vowed to protect her, in any way that was necessary.

After hearing of the private excesses of Silverton, and his beyond reproach business enterprises, Jack realized he was the only one who could bring the man to justice. He had to do it. It was a matter of principle.

There were no more signs of flooding, the thirsty ground having soaked up the water, the heat evaporating the pools of water trapped by rocks.

Cassie had learnt a few things about Jack, and about herself, in the days just past. He'd protected her, and she would always be grateful to him, but the real reason she stayed with him, instead of heading towards the highway on her own, was that she wanted to be with him, wherever he was. It was too soon to call it love. It was more like necessity.

They rode slowly because the ground was rocky, and filled with holes. Having lost her shoes in the flood, Cassie had put on a pair of Jack's thick socks. She was grateful for their horses, it would have been torture to walk with the ground so rough and hot. No wonder lizards lifted one foot at a time as they sped across the sand. Along the journey, there was plenty of time to think.

Cassie had given up thoughts of getting back to America any time soon, but knowing her family would worry, she wished she could contact them. They'd never believe she could take care of herself at this rate.

Back in Nevada she knew how far she could go. The rules of survival there were clear. She could trust her cell phone to work, no matter where she was. The weather was predictable, if you knew what to look for. People were hard to work around, but if you minded your own business, you were left alone.

In Australia the risk was greater. Aussies spoke English, but it was more complicated. Some words were simple, like boot. Cassie knew what a boot was. You put it on your foot. Not so in Australia. Here, a boot was the trunk of your car. It was also on your foot. It had a duel personality.

All she really wanted to do was hunt fossils. They didn't expect anything of you. They just lay in the ground and waited until you dug them up. No drama. They didn't even bite, not like Australia's wild dog, the dingo. She'd heard some stories about them, and always kept a look out, just in case one turned up where she was camping.

Fossils were her reason for coming to this dry, complicated country. Even the floods here were unpredictable. If she left it to Jack, she'd be stuck in the outback without a fossil to her name and the people who were a threat to him would take her down as well.

As she looked at him, riding so confidently, expecting her to follow without question, she started to feel resentful. How would he like it if they were in America, traveling in the wilds of Nevada to places he didn't want to go, forced to travel with someone he didn't know, and didn't even want to know. He would probably be like a fish out of water in Nevada. How would he react if he couldn't understand what the hell people were talking about?

As Cassie's thoughts came back to the journey, wondering how much further they could travel and still not come close to civilization, she made a conscious decision to try to relax for now and take pleasure in the environment. They entered a gorge through rocky hills, walking the horses through a narrow passage made of sandstone, emerging on the other side to find a miracle of abundant plant life.

"This is Morialta Gorge," he explained as they set the horses free in a grassy area close to the water. "It's an Aboriginal word. It means ever-flowing. It has everything we need for a camp, including a natural spring for drinking water."

"No dingoes?"

"I haven't seen any." Jack grinned. "I thought you could deal with anything that came up?"

"Yeah. Sure. I can handle a dinosaur like you can't I? Wild dogs should be a snap."

Jack laughed and rode on. Cassie followed behind, as usual, but her resentment had mellowed. It was hard to be irritated when you were surrounded by such glorious scenery.

They had arrived at a beautiful hidden gorge with the river gently flowing through it, forming a wide pool, perfect for swimming.

"It's paradise, Jack. I love it." The walls were high with a few places where grass had found sanctuary in the rocks. The deep rust and browns were vivid in the sunlight. Trees grew amongst huge rocks, which were higher than the tallest man and scattered around the area like a giant child's marbles. It was an untamed place, full of soft breezes, and indescribable beauty.

After they set their things down, Cassie began to look around. She could see that he had camped here before. A shelter had already been constructed. All they had to do was tidy up a bit and check for eight-legged wildlife.

"Why didn't we come here in the first place?" she asked.

"We couldn't get here because of the flood. Besides, Kalangadoo was where I had to go first. To meet Kev and Blue. This place is safer. I don't think those mongrels know about it. I've built up a stash of tinned and dry food, and instant coffee."

Cassie sighed. "I love fast coffee. I'm desperate for some caffeine."

Jack grinned. "Me too. I've got other supplies too, more soap and first aid supplies. The local Aborigines are the only ones who might come here. This is their land. Somewhere around here are cave paintings, but I've never seen them. I think they deserve to be left in peace. Anyway, I've got other things to think about."

"Yeah. Coffee. I'll get some kindling." Cassie rushed off to collect wood.

Jack wished he could shake off the uneasy feeling he had, that they hadn't seen the last of Kev and Blue. He was locked into a course that might lead to destruction and he didn't want to take Cassie with him. She returned, arms laden with sticks.

"No-one will know we're here, unless they have a helicopter, so you should try to use dry wood for that fire, Cassie. Wet wood makes smoke."

"Yes, boss. I get it. No smoke signals." Cassie looked around, taking in the colors and looking longingly at the water. "So, we'll be alone will we?" Her eyes were shining with anticipation. "Is it safe to swim?"

"Sure. Just have a look around first and make sure there aren't any crocs to nibble at your toes." Jack grinned at the thought. He hoped she wasn't into skinny-dipping. He could be in deep trouble before he knew it.

Cassie looked towards the water, momentarily apprehensive, then looked back with suspicion. "You told me there weren't any crocs this far south."

He tried to look innocent, and failed. "Did I?" he asked. "I'm sure if we looked hard enough we could find a crocodile. Don't worry, I'll protect you?"

Cassie looked down. Her voice was muffled as she said, "I ... um... haven't got a swimsuit. I was looking for dinosaur bones, not beaches." She was remembering how she'd watched him swim at the river, reliving the churning heat she had experienced when she saw him walking naked into the water, and out again.

It didn't help to have him stand within touching distance, enabling her to see the hard muscles of his chest and the strength of his thighs. She longed to reach out and touch him but was afraid of what would surely follow. She had promised she wouldn't stir him up again, and at the time she had meant it, but it was one of the hardest things she had to do in her life.

Cassie wasn't a prude, but she had certain values and a healthy respect for her body. She had no plans to indulge herself in an encounter that could lead to disaster. It was going to be a rocky road if she spent much more time with Jack. He was an enormous temptation.

Hoping her confused feelings didn't show on her face, she ran off, calling back to him, "Last one in is road-kill."

Pulling off his socks and her shirt, she wore her shorts and tank top into the water. By the time he responded to her challenge and reached the bank, she was halfway across the river, swimming as if her life depended on it. He looked after her ruefully. What made her take off like that, he wondered? Anyone would think she was afraid of him.

He had seen the flash of mischief in her gorgeous sherry colored eyes before long dark lashes hid it. Inevitably, his gaze had wandered.

A vee of creamy skin exposed by her shirt had caught

the sun and he'd imagined himself undoing her buttons one by one to expose the valley below. That in turn had led to thoughts of removing the rest of her clothes and ...stop right there Jack!

He gave himself an inward shake and forced himself to think of other things, like whether he was going to swim or not. He decided that he might as well get as comfortable as possible. Although with Cassie around it was going to be of little benefit. He seemed to always feel overheated around her.

Quickly, Jack shed his shorts, shirt, socks and boots. Leaving navy boxer shorts in place, he dived into the water. It was wonderfully cool, soothing. The tension and heat of the day seemed to magically disappear. He swam out a little way, floating, luxuriating in the depth and buoyancy of the ever-flowing river, every now and then reaching down with a foot to touch the sand on the riverbed. It was coarse and grainy, and he rubbed his toes through it, feeling it massage his feet beautifully.

Suddenly he was pushed under the water and came up spluttering and coughing in an attempt to clear his nose and mouth of water. He wiped his face and beard with his hands and shook back his lion's mane of hair.

Instantly he swooped upon the girl who had ducked him, catching hold of her, and then wrapping his arms around her waist. She struggled, but was laughing so hard that he held on to her easily, her supple flesh firm and inviting.

They went under the water, each trying to control the other. In the finish, Jack won. Not because of his superior strength and size, but because he played dirty.

He kissed her under the water and they came to the surface still joined, mouths locked together, arms holding each other as if they had been welded together like bronze statues.

Desire flared between them as their bare legs tangled, friction generating an explosive heat, which entered every pore of their breathless bodies.

Cassie could think of nothing but how much she wanted this man. She felt as if she had just been born, and he was the only thing that could ensure her survival in a world gone insane. All her fears, of Silverton, of Blue and Kev, of the police operation, disappeared as if they had never been.

Jack knew she belonged to him, and in that moment he was lost. He needed to make her his woman, permanently and for all time. It took a few minutes for the memory of her inexperience to kick in and he eased away with regret.

He wasn't usually the type of man who lost control, but the woman in his arms was all he had ever wanted. That made him want to protect her, not only from animals like Kev and Blue, but from men like himself who could hurt her without intent.

His voice was hoarse as he said, "Cassie, darling, I think we should cool off a little. I don't want you to do anything you'll regret, okay?"

She blushed at the 'edge-of-control' note in his voice, knowing that he was right. They had got carried away and she was grateful that he had called a halt when he did.

At the same time she felt a tingle of resentment. Irrationally, she had wanted him to lose control, wanted him to act out the primitive fantasies she had woven about him making love to her. She needed him to be oblivious to anything but her.

Knowing the right and sensible thing to do was one thing, doing it was something else. She had discovered in herself a fierce desire to know Jack, in every way there is. But he had refused to take what had been offered.

Illogically she thought, I won't offer again. If he wants me, he'll have to come on bended knee, and beg. Even then I might say no. But she knew deep down that she was lying to herself. If he asked, she would give him anything he asked for, and more.

Over the next few days, Jack stayed away from Cassie as much as possible. He had things he needed to work out. It was all he could do not to grab her like a caveman, and drag her to a grassy spot near the river, giving her what her amber eyes had been unconsciously pleading for.

The problem was, he wanted it too. Desperately. But he was unprepared for a physical relationship. There could be repercussions. For both their sakes he had to hold back and allow the situation to cool down. Their time would come he vowed, but not yet. At the moment his business was on hold, his life a tangle of police, drugs and brutality.

As dawn broke one morning, a few days after they reached the gorge, Cassie woke up and decided to take a swim, and wash her hair. She gathered up some soap, a towel and a blanket to wrap herself in while her clothes dried.

Since she had lost her pack, she had to make do with Jack's shirt on the days she cleaned her clothes. Unfortunately this day he was wearing it.

Down at the water, she carefully looked around before stripping off and wading into the cool water. Jack had been in his sleeping bag when she left, so she felt quite safe to swim and wash her clothes at the same time.

After swimming back and forth from one side of the river to the other, Cassie climbed out onto a grassy bank on the far side. It was out of sight of their camp, trees grew at the water's edge. Large boulders, a prominent feature of the area, made the spot she chose a perfect place to dry off unobserved. As it was early in the day the sun wasn't at full strength, but she was still careful not to stay too long exposed.

She lay face down on the grass and felt the warmth of the morning sun touching her naked body like a sun-shower, each valley and curve responding to it like a lover's kiss.

It was the closest she had ever been to pure physical pleasure, except for the times when Jack had taken her in his arms and kissed her. That didn't mean she was going to do anything about it she assured herself, thinking in her innocence that she was in control of the situation. She hadn't yet realized how a person's strength of will could be swept away by the blind need to be loved by, and make love with, the beloved.

Cassie didn't understand that the emotion he aroused in her was love. Her body knew, but her mind stubbornly refused to admit it. She thought what she felt was merely sexual, and when she went back to Nevada, it would be a case of 'out of sight, out of mind'. She forgot she had rejected almost every male in her own group of friends at home. All they thought about was making money and how they looked in their business suits. Jack would look good in one too, she was sure, if he trimmed his beard and long hair.

Although she was fiercely independent, deep down where her heart dreamed Cassie wanted someone to love her. She loved children and secretly hoped to be able to have a family of her own.

She fell asleep, under the shade of a gum tree, dreaming of Jack. He was making love to her, taking her to a place she had never been before. It was heaven.

Jack had swum across the river and climbed out, not realizing that an exquisitely shaped girl would be lying naked like an offering to the Gods. He had carefully stayed away from her as much as possible in order to protect her from himself. But now, here she was, asleep in the shade of gum trees and rocks, the sun dappling her skin, one arm flung to the side, her cheek resting on her other arm, her soft skin glowing with a healthy sheen. He stood there for a moment, spellbound by her natural beauty and long, shining copper hair. It was magic.

What he really needed right now was a long cold shower, something to freeze him in his tracks. There was only so much a man could take, and he had reached his limit. It wouldn't do for her to wake up and find him there, staring at her like a voyeur.

A moment later, Cassie rolled over and all Jack's good intentions went out the window. He stepped forward, reaching down to run his fingers over the slope of her breast. It was soft to the touch, and before he knew it, he was encircling it with his whole hand, stroking the nipple into abundant life.

He heard a gasp, and the encounter became tense as Cassie moved away slightly, not breaking contact, but quivering with anticipation. For a moment he couldn't move. Time stood still as he watched and waited for her to make a move, either toward him, or away.

She reached out her hand and touched his face, watching him as he paused, silently urging him to continue his exploration. As he sighed and moved closer she put her arms around him, then ran her fingers through his hair. "Jack," she whispered. "Make love to me. I need you."

Jack groaned. How could he resist her when she was so giving, so accepting of him. She didn't protest as he moved over her, the passion of his kiss a prelude to making her his. She could not resist as he put his arms around her fully and lowered his now naked body against her own hungering warmth.

Touching him, stroking her hands across his chest, and down to the evidence of his desire, was the greatest pleasure she had ever known. Seeing the man in the flesh was one thing. Touching him was altogether different. She never wanted it to end. Then he touched her, his hands traveling where no one had gone before. It was the preparation for heaven.

As he slipped into her quivering flesh, Jack realized that this was the place he wanted to be. Nothing in his previous life had prepared him for such an experience. He wanted it to go on, and on. And it did.

Cassie sighed with completion. Any slight discomfort at his penetration was now a distant memory. If she had known it was such an incredible thing to make love, she wouldn't have waited so long. Jack touched her face with a gentle hand then withdrew from her, and somehow she knew it would take her forever to forget how wonderful it felt to have him inside her.

He closed his eyes, and said, "I shouldn't have done that. I didn't take precautions."

To Cassie, it was like a cold shower. "I didn't have anything either, Jack. You weren't alone in this." Her eyes filled with tears.

"But it was your first time. I should have been more responsible."

Cassie blushed. "It was my choice. I could have said no. I didn't. End of story." She moved further away from him and stood up, picking up a towel from the rocks at her feet.

He wanted to protest as she shielded her body from his eyes.

"Why didn't you?" he asked.

"I didn't want to. Anyway, it had to happen some time.

If anything happens, I'll let you know" She stood up and walked to the water, quickly dropping the towel and submerging her whole body. She didn't look at Jack. If she had, the hurt he was feeling would have been clear.

Jack hated to see her go, but knew it was the best thing. Otherwise he'd be making love to her again, compounding the problem.

He knew he must be strong. It was difficult though, and would get more difficult before they could leave this place with its abundant temptations. He silently groaned in despair before going into the water himself, deciding that self-sacrifice was not something he was good at. It was torture.

Watching Cassie swim a slight distance away, Jack called out to her. "Cassie, before you get too far away, I need to make sure you understand how hazardous it would be if you try to leave here."

She pushed her wet hair out of her eyes and swam back toward him. "I know it's dangerous, Jack. You don't have to keep rubbing it in."

He sighed. "I don't think you understand. This gorge is safe. It's well hidden and no one knows about it. The trouble is, if you leave without me, you could be seen. I won't be able to protect you."

"Don't worry. I'll stay in the gorge. It's a beautiful place. You go on and look for your plants or whatever it is you had planned. I'll be okay."

Cassie smiled at him then sank underneath the water. She surfaced a distance away and watched as he waded to the shore. She liked that he was worried about her. Maybe they had a future after all.

Jack decided to take her at her word. It was time to get down to business anyway and he couldn't delay it any longer. It was better that Cassie wasn't further involved. She would be okay staying by herself he decided, safer than if he stayed with her at camp. She was rapidly becoming an obsession; he had no choice but to diffuse the situation before it became too hard to control.

He consoled himself with the fact that didn't really know each other. Camouflage had become a habit with each of them, he with his shaggy hair and rough clothes, she with her temper and I-don't-give-a-damn attitude. They had forgotten that nature makes its own rules and has its own solutions.

When Cassie arrived back at camp after her swim, she found Jack's note on her sleeping bag. He said he had something to do and would return later. Deciding she might as well take the time to explore her surroundings, she put on her hat.

To call the gorge beautiful was to understate its impact on the senses. It was the overwhelming variety of color and the intoxicating perfume from native trees that made her wish she could stay forever. The golden backed honeyeater seemed to agree as it hunted for insects, and sang high in the branches of a eucalyptus tree.

Following a path leading into tangled undergrowth, pushing aside scrubby trees and prickly grasses, Cassie came across a rocky outcrop. A narrow path next to the river led to a track wide enough for a vehicle. It was overgrown and looked as if it had been used very little of late. She walked along it hoping to find another way out of the area. The path had no direct access to the gorge, it seemed to taper off into rocks, but it could be from anywhere, possibly from a road that led to the Plenty Highway.

The sun was glaring down; it's enervating rays heating the earth. Perspiration was gathering on Cassie's face by the time she stopped, she drank a little of her water bottle's contents as she rested, her shirt sticking to her back. Jack's socks were on her feet still, but were now threadbare. She'd have to buy him a new pair.

Strange, she thought, he said the only way to the gorge was the rock tunnel they had entered by. Perhaps he wasn't aware of the track she now followed, or maybe, evil thought, he had lied to her.

She shoved that nasty idea into the back of her mind as being too uncomfortable to pursue at that moment. Later she could have another look and see what it meant. It could just be he had forgotten to tell her. He did have a lot on his mind.

Cassie kept walking, finding another path, which led, over a hill, into another valley. Trees and undergrowth made it impossible to see far ahead There was a dirt track, clearly in use, and tire tracks. Wondering if this was the way to Jack's field lab, she followed the track to a bend, where it branched out into two. As she took the right hand track, she heard voices. What was going on? Was that Jack? And someone else as well? Maybe Silverton had turned up?

Cassie could hear the voices quite clearly so she slowed her walk, easing into a curve of the track, stepping softly around some large rocks and mulga trees with thick foliage. She saw four men. Three were strangers; dressed like businessmen. Wearing wide brimmed hats, they were leaning against a late model SUV, drinking beer.

Jack was the fourth man, standing apart from the others. He looked confident, but there was a tension about him that made Cassie catch her breath. She could see it in the set of his shoulders.

She flattened herself behind a tree, keeping out of sight, listening.

"We got your message, Doc." The voice was smooth, cultured. Who was Doc, she wondered? Oh, yes, that was

Jack, she remembered he'd told her he had a PhD in pharmacognosy, 'It's in the dictionary', he'd said when she laughed. "Ive got a stack of letters after my name. I made them up too."

"I take it Blue and Kev caught up with you?"

Cassie realized this must be Silverton talking. "Yes. Kev spun a tale about you and a woman giving him a hard time."

"Yeah. So what?"

"I don't give a toss. All I want is the goods. Blue and Kev can say what they like. Doesn't matter. I already know they're liars, thieves and gamblers. That's why I employ them. Never trust an honest man. He'll turn you in to the law at the drop of a hat. Blue and Kev are mine, they owe me big time. End of story."

"Where are they?"

"Back at Jasper Creek. They stole a jeep from a mining camp."

"Very resourceful," said Jack. "Are they in jail?"

Silverton said, "They didn't get caught. I didn't come here to chat, Blackwood. I came to check on my investment."

"The plants aren't mature yet. Why don't I call you when they're ready?"

"I'd rather look now. I can take copies of the research with me today. Save us all a lot of bother. Don't forget the location map."

Jack frowned. "If you come when I call you, everything will be ready and I'll make sure no-one's around. The place will be empty."

Silverton was silent for a moment, then he said, "Okay. We'll come back. But know this, Blackwell, I'm not happy. If you've got that woman hanging around, she's a liability. Get rid of her. I want that research. You want the money. That's the deal."

Jack said, "That was the deal. I told Kev to pass the message on. If you want this to go ahead, I want to be paid in advance. Add another zero to the amount as well."

Cassie gasped. What was he doing? Silverton wouldn't go for that. She was right. He didn't. "You trying to shaft me, Blackwood?"

"Call it a bonus for stress caused by Kev and Blue. I'm going in to Jasper Creek tomorrow. I'll leave a letter for you at the hotel. My account details will be on it."

Silverton's face was hard. He said, "Another deal. I pay in advance, but no extra cash. Otherwise forget it."

Jack waited for a moment, and then he said, "Done."

Jack had been instructed by the police to lead Silverton along, playing the camel trader to make him think Jack was a dealer. Silverton fell for it and the trap was set.

Silverton and his men climbed into their SUV and drove away. Jack walked in the other direction before Cassie could call out to him. Then she decided to go back to the gorge and wait for him. She had quite a lot to say about his handling of the situation.

Cassie sat on a rock back at camp, thinking about what she had heard. She decided to ask Jack outright what was going on. What was that about money being put in his account? Something didn't add up. Still that subliminal trust she had for Jack persisted, against all odds, and at last, alone in the waiting silence of Morialta Gorge, Cassie acknowledged to herself the truth. She trusted him because she wanted to, because she needed to. To do otherwise was to betray herself.

Eight

Alone with her fears and doubts, Cassie eventually became restless and decided to go looking for the man who had turned her life upside down. Where had Jack gone? She walked along the path next to the rocky outcrop and on to the bush track outside Morialta Gorge. A little further on, the track widened on to a flat, sandy area near a sandstone cliff. There were tire tracks, but no sign of Jack.

There was however another kind of dinosaur she could be looking for. Some of the rocks had evidence of tiny sea creatures layered into them. If she looked deeper, she might find something larger, or hard evidence, like bones. As she looked at the sandstone cliff above her, she decided to find a way to climb. Up high, she could get a better view of the area and see if there were any places where caves could be hidden. Thinking about her futile encounter with Jack, and wondering what went wrong, wasn't finding her proof of sea creatures or dinosaurs in the center of the Australian outback.

And which was more important? The end, or the beginning? The most riveting pleasurable encounter of her life was over. Strike that. The only pleasurable encounter of her life, was over. Her career as a respected paleontologist was just beginning. There was no comparison. Her whole life was on hold until she found what she was looking for. Jack obviously wasn't it, so it was time to move on.

Where to move on to was the problem. She kept thinking back to Jack, and the mess his life had become. All her doubts had risen to the surface; she sensed something dangerous was going to happen. She hoped he would keep his head down but knew he would be the first to jump into the line of fire. He wasn't a man to sit back and wait for something to happen. He'd make it happen so he could control it.

Walking on a little further, Cassie found that the track, which had been partially cleared, came around in a semi-circle, stopping in a clearing. She wondered if Silverton had come here with his SUV. If he had, it wasn't here now. When she walked towards the sandstone cliff face, planning to look at the wildflowers growing nearby, she found, to her astonishment, part of the rock wall moved. A slight breeze had begun to skim through the trees and had sent what was supposed to be solid rock into a ripple of movement.

She stopped in her tracks, convinced that the heat was causing her to have hallucinations. Then the breeze picked up considerably and the wall undulated, flapping about, making a cracking noise like the sail on a yacht. She jumped at the sound.

Upon closer investigation, Cassie found part of the rock wall to be a carefully constructed curtain of painted canvas. Even at close range, it looked to be reddish sandstone, but instead it was an expensive piece of camouflage.

Carefully, she moved the cloth aside, discovering the entrance to a cave. It was dark, she couldn't see very far, but there seemed to be things stored in there. Just inside she found a panel of switches hooked up on the rock wall, one of which lit up the whole of a large cavern.

Cassie was astonished. There were shelves containing

laboratory equipment and tools. Tins of food were stacked up against one wall, bags of fertilizer on the floor. Fertilizer? Must be for Jack's plants. Seemed like overkill for a few poppies, but what did she know. She dug things up, not planted them.

Water containers took up space. There was also a door built into an inside rock wall. A large, heavy-duty padlock prevented her from opening it and exploring. Best of all, there was an SUV. What a find!

Feeling shell-shocked, Cassie turned the lights off and came outside. It must be powered by a solar panel somewhere, she thought, as she sat on a rock in the clearing, staring at the canvas curtain. I wonder why Jack didn't tell me about this?

That thought was the worm in the apple. He must know about the cave, the SUV and equipment must be his. He could have driven her to Jasper Creek or even Alice Springs any time he liked. But he hadn't.

What a rat, a low down, conniving, lying rat. Perhaps he really was doing something illegal? Stashing away money in offshore accounts maybe? Thoughts went round and round in her head until she nearly screamed with it. How could life be so unfair?

She was becoming more and more attached to that great bear of a man, now she found he had betrayed her, stringing her along like a fool. So much for trust.

She had thought something was fishy when she heard him ask Silverton to pay money into his account. This was an emotional turmoil. She didn't want him to be one of the bad guys.

In her heart she had hoped and dreamed he would turn out to be a prince, instead she was discovering that frogs can look like princes on the outside, but inside they still croak and slurp flies.

Seeing the evidence of her misplaced love before her eyes, Cassie took a long look inside herself. She had dreamed of finding a man who was honest, and who loved her as much as she loved him. Now her dreams had turned to dust.

I'm not staying in this primitive nest of vipers, she thought savagely. I've had enough of lies and half-truths. I'm going back to Nevada, where I can be myself. Everyone there knows I'm an up front kind of person, a girl who calls it like it is. If they don't like who I am, too bad. Maybe I'll find myself a man who likes caving and digging up bones. We could do it together. We could do other things together too. And this time we'd both know what we were getting into. Each other.

The trouble with that was, there was no one like Jack. He was a hard act to follow.

After a moment, she calmed down enough to allow the eternal optimist to pop its head up, reminding herself that, with incentives, people can change. Maybe Jack could change into a man who could communicate, a person who let other people into his life. If he did, she would be waiting, but not forever. There were bones to be found, a reputation to be built. Achieving that would take determination.

She decided to go back to camp and wait, tackling him when he returned. It was getting late in the day and she was hungry. It was fire season all year round here, and Jack said they shouldn't light a fire to boil water, unless they were desperate, so a can of fruit would have to do. Cassie enjoyed living on the land, but some things, like electric ovens, gas fires, refrigerators and soft beds were hard to live without. A washing machine would have been nice too. She could live without a dryer. A clothesline strung from tree to tree would have been fine, but she didn't even have a piece of rope.

Anyway, smoke would be a beacon for trouble. Anyone could follow the trail in the air and find them. The smell of smoke would make it even easier. Being found was not something either of them wanted.

Maybe Jack was back already? There was probably more than one way into Morialta Gorge. All she had to do was explore, and maybe she'd find it.

She hurried down the track and through the narrow rocky path towards their camp, hoping he would listen and give up anything illegal he was involved in.

To Cassie's intense disappointment, Jack wasn't there.

She paced back and forth for a while, the tension building until she thought she would burst if she couldn't talk to him. Then, feeling hot and tense, she took a swim in her underwear, hoping he wouldn't return until she had finished. Swimming naked would be tempting fate, and Jack. While she would welcome another chance to make love with him, it was dangerous to get used to it. They still didn't have any protection, and she knew he would move on. She just didn't know if she would be invited to go too.

It seemed that danger surrounded them. Jack had said he wanted to keep her safe, but wasn't she safe with him? He was a man of two minds. One moment he brushed her off, telling her to keep away, the next he was making love to her, showing her how wonderful it would be if they stayed together.

If they talked, maybe she could get the real picture, instead of the scraps of information he decided to pass on. Then she could make up her own mind.

After she had dried herself and dressed again, she brushed her long hair until it dried, a shining tumble of copper curls. She still wanted to look her best. If he refused to tell her the truth about what was going on, she wanted him to know what he was going to be missing.

It was nearly time for a meal by the time he returned and, shaking nervously, she went to him as soon as he arrived, intending to confront him with her suspicions.

Before she could speak, however, he said distractedly, "Cassie. I don't have time to talk to you now; I have to go off again for day or so. You'll be okay won't you?"

"What do you care?" Cassie turned away from him, and he realized he had hurt her badly.

The look on her face was painful. Jack realized he was causing her distress, leaving her alone, but what could he do. He was between a rock and a hard place. If he didn't go, the whole mission he was involved in would fall in a heap, and he had come too far to let that happen. Cassie would just have to understand. She couldn't be involved in any way. He would rather abort the whole thing than put her in danger, but if he terminated the operation before a result was achieved, there would be more than Cassie's safety at stake. There would be other people involved, other lives at risk. He couldn't take that chance.

He said, "I care, Cassie. You don't know how much, but I don't have a choice."

Without waiting for an answer, he hurriedly started to fill his backpack with supplies, saying over his shoulder, "Don't leave the gorge will you? It's safer here, and I should be back in two days at the most." He gave her a quick hug and began to walk away, already somewhere else in his mind.

She ran after him and said, "But Jack, I want to talk to you. It's important!"

"It'll have to wait. Sorry, love, I'm in too much of a hurry. We'll have lots to talk about when I get back, okay? See you later." Before she could say anything else, he strode off into the bush, leaving Cassie prey to doubts and misgivings.

Surely, if he cared about her at all, he would have taken the time to listen. She slumped in despair. What was she going to do now? She just hoped he wasn't doing something dangerous, or illegal. That worm in the apple was getting bigger and bigger.

She stood up, shaking her head. No, she wasn't going to be treated as if she was just a pointless distraction in the important scheme of things. Jack would have to learn she had a will of her own. It was time to see to her own needs.

The camp began to seem like a prison as she packed her things. She wanted to go, immediately. The problem was, Jack wasn't there to tell. Then she realized. He was really gone. Waiting around to tell him she was going was pointless. The danger of Jack's drug enterprise was too much to handle. It was time to cut and run, but where to run to was the problem? Added to that it was getting dark. There were creatures out there, cliffs for her to fall down, rivers for her to drown in. She couldn't go anywhere until the sun came up.

After stewing all night, thinking about Gerald Silverton and his drugs, worrying and wondering about Jack and the hidden cave, she decided she'd run out of patience. Enough was enough.

She missed her family and friends. She needed work in order to finance her expeditions. Paleontology projects awaited her, especially discoveries in Nevada. There were Lehman Caves in the Great Basin National Park to explore. There was a wealth of material to discover in the rock formations hidden in the back of the caves. Bones and fossils were everywhere and her skills were necessary to recognize them and record their existence, to map the lifeline of planet earth. That was her expertise, what she had studied for all her life. She was needed, and nothing was going to stop her fulfilling her destiny. Not even her primal man who could make her forget her own name just by touching her and taking her in his arms, kissing her trembling lips. She wasn't going to put them aside for the sake of a man who didn't care about her, who wouldn't even listen or answer her questions, a man who might be more involved with drug trafficking than even the police realized.

After cleaning her coffee cup in the river, Cassie made her way to the cave and pulled the canvas curtain aside. The place was still deserted, thank goodness. She looked around for a key, elated when she found one hanging near the light panel at the entrance. Jack always told her never to leave her key in the ignition of a car. He was paranoid about thieves, although why he bothered in the wilderness she didn't' know. Maybe it was just a habit he had developed hanging around with criminals.

She loaded food and water from supplies in the cave into the back of the SUV and climbed into the drivers seat. Thank heaven she had become familiar with Australian vehicles, with the steering wheel on the right hand side.

The key was unfamiliar, but she persisted with some colorful adjectives and finally the steering lock gave and she managed to start the engine. It sounded like a roar in the hollow cave. She looked around nervously in case anyone was close enough to hear, and try to prevent her leaving. After all, she didn't know who might be around; all she knew was that Jack was gone.

Quickly, Cassie backed past the canvas curtain, and out of the cave, turning the vehicle on to the overgrown track. Almost free she thought breathlessly as she stepped on the gas.

She had been driving slowly and carefully for about

half an hour when the track ended at a slightly wider and more used road. After turning west, toward Alice Springs, the small track could not be seen. Undergrowth and trees concealed it. Just in case she came back this way, she stopped and marked the nearest tree with a piece of red cloth used as a rag in the toolbox. It was a small piece of insurance.

The gorge had no indication of its existence showing to the outside world, except by aerial surveillance. Jack had said it was a hidden place, unknown to casual passers by. The maps and aerial photographs of the area he'd shown her were in her bag and she had studied them carefully. What would he say when he found she'd disappeared, and so had his SUV?

He could be completely innocent, or he could be a liar. There was no way to tell, so she shrugged off such speculation as pointless and depressing, putting her foot down hard as she sped away towards Jasper Creek.

It was time she cut her losses and took control of her life again, instead of being manipulated. If Jack were an honest man, he'd have told her about the cave and explained what was going on with the money from Silverton. If he were one of the bad guys, he would be kicking himself at letting her escape.

She felt savagely triumphant as she drove away. There would be no more swimming together, no more cooking over campfires, no more laughter, especially no more gullible females. And, there would be no more vehicles for him to use. He'd have to find some other means to get to town. She hoped he got as many blisters on his feet as she had that day they met, when she had been forced to hurry along in his footsteps.

Then she remembered the police. They'd probably pick him up. If Jack had fooled them too, Cassie hoped justice and truth would prevail.

As she approached Jasper Creek, Cassie's mood of recrimination and anger lessened to a feeling of deep regret and sadness. How he could have fooled her as he had done was something she couldn't understand. She had trusted him.

She made a silent vow that she would be less trusting. She'd look out for people like him in the future and run the other way. She would make the rules from now on. And if she decided to break those rules, well, that was her choice.

Jack had seemed to like her, treating her as if he had a genuine regard for her. He'd even kissed her as if he meant it. It just proved to her how naive she was. She knew he'd be angry she'd disappeared, but hoped to be long gone before he arrived in Jasper Creek. It's the best way, she told herself, and then I won't ever have to see him again.

She was forced to pull over at that point to calm herself, her eyes filled with useless tears, even on an empty road you had to see where you were going or you'd end up bogged in mud or hitting a kangaroo.

The Australian outback has no time for fools or dreamers. It can dispose of your life in an instant or put it on hold for a very long time.

She thought of her aborted trip to the dig at Alcoota. It had been the guiding force in her life up to the point when she'd met Jack, a stepping-stone to more significant discoveries. Now that he was potentially out of the picture, she would concentrate on more worthwhile things.

Just before she'd left America, there had been wonderful scientific news of paleontologists finding the bones of a diprotodon here in Australia. It was like a giant wombat. The cranial capacity was small, so it had a small brain, and probably wasn't very intelligent. In that case, the diprotodon had something in common with Blue Murphy. Kev O'Shannassy was another matter entirely. He was smart but vicious. By all accounts, the diprotodon was a peaceful herbivore.

Cassie decided; if she could get a work permit in Australia and do paid work on a dig she might even give up library work. It would be much more to her taste, digging and caving and living in the Aussie outback. Something about this country called to her. It was wild, and free, and you could see the stars at night without breathing exhaust fumes.

There was also the possibility of going to the cave where the diprotodon bones had been found, although the cave had been previously covered over to make way for a camping park. Limekiln cave was where a lost lake was found; cave experts diving for hidden treasures. Not gold or jewels but prehistoric bones. These were found with evidence that people were present when they died. It was a remarkable discovery, and Cassie wanted to go there. There might also be the aquatic evidence she was searching for. With caves, there was usually water, and there could be sea creatures hidden in the depths.

That afternoon, when Cassie arrived in Jasper Creek, she was exhausted and emotionally drained. It had been a long journey through searing heat, the rough, scrub-covered hills and red, dusty plains demanding total concentration. Gritty, sore eyes and a headache didn't make for a comfortable or safe journey.

Surely Jack could have taken some time from his busy schedule to bring her to civilization. It wasn't as though it was on the other side of the world, not like America. Maybe his agenda didn't allow for side trips to help a friend, or a lover. Not that she was a real lover. More like a temporary fling in the desert, a detour. His criminal enterprise was obviously more important.

Heated air shimmered on the flat black tar of the highway; vinyl seats burned tender flesh. The white SUV was covered with a thick layer of dust. She'd seen no other vehicles on the road and could have been on Mars, except for the vast cobalt blue sky, white cockatoos and gum trees fighting for survival in dry creek beds.

After parking on a side street, next to a garage, Cassie sat for a moment. Thanking God for a gum tree and a tiny patch of shade, she almost fell into the roadway, throat parched with dust, bones aching with the weariness of sitting for hours.

The wide main street of the outback town was silent. Tiny dust-filled whirlwinds flew where they would, allowing the rust-brown cattle dog by the hotel door the freedom to sleep through the afternoon, undisturbed, even by flies or fleas.

Cassie didn't dare go into the hotel. Silverton had said Kev and Blue were free in Jasper Creek? Seeing them would be a disaster. The town seemed deserted, even though it was mid week, then she saw an open sign on the general store. She could buy something to eat.

That's if they accepted credit cards. She could buy clothes, a new pack, and a shoulder bag at the store. She could look civilized again. A shower wouldn't be hard to take either, but such luxuries would have to wait. The money belt her father had insisted on giving her hadn't been lost in the flood. She had got into the habit of keeping it hidden from everyone. Keeping your belongings under lock and key was paramount. It was too bad she hadn't kept her body under lock and key. Then she wouldn't have regrets about making love with Jack. The flip side was, she wouldn't have had any memories either. On balance, she decided she would rather have the memories. At least they would keep her warm at night.

The visa card sign on the dusty store door was reassuring and Cassie felt relieved. The outback wasn't anywhere near as primitive as it seemed in the brochures. Not all of it, anyway.

After she had shopped, she took her food to a small shady park. It was cooler than in the sun and, as she ate, she looked through a folder of papers she had found in the glove compartment of Jack's SUV, justifying her snooping by telling herself, what Jack had done to her was just as bad. He'd lied to her, and then left her. What could be worse than that?

There was a driver's license in the name of Dr. Jason Blackwood, with an address in Melbourne and a tiny photograph of a handsome, short haired, clean shaven man she assumed was Jack, although it was hard to tell since he wore glasses.

As well, there was an insurance certificate and vehicle ownership papers both made out in the same name and several business cards giving the name of a pharmaceutical research establishment. At least that part was the truth.

Cassie thought back to her first impressions of Jack. She'd thought he was poor, living rough. Then she'd learned about his pharmaceutical research company. He was probably wealthier than her parents. She thought about his worn clothes and how she had wished he would clean himself up a bit. He must have been laughing at her behind her back for weeks.

She realized now, he probably hadn't made love to her when they first met, not out of respect for her inexperience, but because he was used to more sophisticated women. She was unable to stem the tide of depression when she remembered how she had fallen so hard for him. It would take time to recover, but she would do it, there was no other choice.

Scooping up the papers, Cassie shoved them into her bag, putting them out of her mind. It was time to move on. Maybe distance would help her forget. Home in Nevada began to look like the best place to be. But maybe she could just stop at the dinosaur digs on the way.

She'd go down into a cave, and forget all about men and deception. She'd look for fossils, dig up bones, and be with people who were doing something worthwhile.

After leaving the keys to Jack's vehicle under the driver's seat, she gathered up her few belongings, bought extra water, coffee and a sandwich at a truck stop. Then she spoke to the garage proprietor. "I need a lift to Alice Springs," she told him. "Do you know of any trucks going that way soon?"

"Well, if you wait a bit, there's sure to be somethin' comin' through." He glanced at the SUV and said curiously, "What about the vehicle? The SUV. Isn't that yours?"

"It belongs to a friend of mine. He'll pick it up later." Cassie pulled herself together, giving him a smile to head him off. She had lied about the dusty SUV, not wanting the man to become curious and investigate further, or perhaps write down the license plate and tell the police about it. It was a good thing she hadn't washed the dust off the plate. After all, she had stolen the vehicle. Jack might call the cops. They could keep her there for ages, asking questions she had no answers for. She could find herself in an outback jail awaiting a hearing. That would really put her parents in a spin.

Cassie had told another untruth. Jack wasn't her friend, not any more. Even if he were innocent, he wouldn't appreciate her stealing his vehicle. It was against her principles to deceive people, and she wished she could get out of Jasper Creek before it became necessary to do it again.

After about an hour, a huge cattle truck rumbled to a stop in the main street next to the garage gas pumps. The noise of the diesel engines could be heard rumbling for quite a while after she heard the air brakes take hold. The driver climbed out of his cab, and had walked around to enter the garage office in the side street, when she approached him. She said, "Hello. Nice day isn't it? Look, I need to get to Alice Springs. Would you be headed that way?"

"That's where I'm goin'," he agreed. "You're welcome to ride along with me as far as the depot. Be nice to have someone to talk to besides the yahoos who come on over the CB. Bunch of jokers, some of 'em. Don't know when to shut up."

He grinned sheepishly, as if he was unused to talking, and slapped his dusty hat against a bare brawny thigh. He was a large man but his blue eyes had a curiously innocent look to them. Not like Jack's she thought savagely. She had thought he was trustworthy, but look how she had been deceived.

Cassie smiled uncertainly, looking towards the middle-aged garage owner who had come out to talk to the driver. He said reassuringly, "It'll be okay. Tom can take care of you. He's a bit rough round the edges, but you can trust him."

The brawny truck driver, hearing the garage owner's reassuring words, gave a self-conscious laugh. "I'm goin' over to the pub for a bite. I'll be set to take off again after that." He looked uncertain, and then asked, "Do ya want to come and get something yourself? It's not bad food, and the beer is good and cold. Don't worry. I'm not drinking. You need all your wits about you with a rig like that."

Cassie shuddered at the thought of all the eyes that would dissect her if she entered the pub with the truck driver. It would be like announcing to the world that she was a hitchhiker and questions would be asked.

It was hard to think up a convincing story, so she said, "I've already had some food. Thanks all the same. If you don't mind, I'll just have a little walk around until you're ready. Don't worry about me, I'll be fine."

The truck driver shrugged his huge shoulders. "Okay, if that's the way you want it. I'll be half an hour or so." He turned and ambled across the wide street into the hotel, its wide verandah sheltering the doors from the sun.

After walking back to the park for a while, then looking in the general store window, Cassie strolled past the hotel, forgetting her need to keep out of sight. She was passing the glass entrance door when she looked in and almost fainted with shock. Jack was sitting with a woman in a corner of the bar, a very attractive woman. He'd combed his hair and looked reasonably civilized.

He appeared to be having an intimate conversation, and didn't look up to see the weary redhead who quickly ducked out of sight along the verandah.

It was too much for Cassie to handle. He had deceived her, and now he had a woman with him. Not just any woman either, she was beautiful, pale blonde hair, young. She was looking at him as if he were the answer to every prayer she had ever uttered. Cassie had seen her place her hand on Jack's tanned forearm. She remembered herself doing the same thing, as if she couldn't help but touch him.

Cassie ran across the street, and around the side of the

cattle truck. It was parked next to a shady tree there and she could wait for the driver without being seen from the pub, in case Jack happened to look out. Not that he would, she thought. He's so busy with that woman he won't see anything else. I could probably prance into the bar half naked and he wouldn't even notice. The smell of the steers shifting restlessly in the back of the truck was overwhelming, the heat and the flies making it impossible to breathe. She was still fuming when the truck driver returned to his rig. The steers seemed to know it was time to move and they began to turn around, bodies slamming together, their voices raised in protest at the delay. Cassie thought, 'you guys wouldn't be in such a hurry if you knew where you were going.'

The driver said, "Ready to roll then? Is that all you've got with you?"

"Yeah, that's all. Thanks." He took her shoulder bag and pack from her, hurled it up into the cabin, and then took her hand, helping her up into the high seat of the truck as if she were royalty. She grinned. Some Aussie truck drivers might look rough but underneath they've got hearts of gold.

Cassie looked towards the hotel as the truck started down the street, and her face went white. There he was, coming out of the hotel with that woman, striding along the verandah as if he owned it. She looked as if she belonged by his side. They were both tall and well built with an air of confidence that was entirely natural.

He looked so familiar to Cassie that she almost cried out to him. Then she remembered what he had done, and how confused she felt. How had he got to town anyway? For that matter, why hadn't he asked her to come too?

Then there was the fact that she had stolen his vehicle, and was in the process of escaping from him. Without hesitation, she hunched down in her seat, peeping over the rim of the truck window. It was the only sensible thing to do.

Jack turned then and she ducked down even further. The truck sped down the unsealed road with clouds of dust billowing behind, Jack never even knowing Cassie was on board. It was a good thing the truck driver was busy with his gear changes, she could find nothing of interest to say. Her only comfort was in knowing Jack hadn't seen her.

They reached Alice Springs around ten that night. Cassie thanked the truck driver for the ride, and found a room at a motel. She took a shower, then collapsed, exhausted to sink into a restless sleep.

After a bad night, at least Cassie knew she wasn't pregnant. That would have been a disaster. How would she tell her parents if that had happened. They would never understand. To her father, she was still a little girl. He'd buy a shotgun and catch the first flight to Australia. Jack would have to run and hide.

Somehow she couldn't see that happening. If nothing else, he would stand up and face the consequences of his actions, if there were any.

With mixed feelings, called her parents to let them know she was okay. They were anxious to know where their daughter had been, what had happened to her and when she was coming home. She filled them in as much as possible, but on the subject of Jack, she remained silent. There was a lot she had to leave out. It had been a good while since Cassie had felt able to confide in her family. She knew they loved her, but her life seemed to be going in a different direction from the one they envisaged for her. Jack was too new and painful a subject. She didn't know how to explain how she felt. The hollow feeling of having left something of value behind had been with her throughout the entire journey.

She thought of Jack now, wondering how he was, whether he had noticed his SUV in the side street, and retrieved it without reporting her to the police.

Then she remembered what he had done to her and started brooding again. There was also the memory of him standing with that woman outside the pub. Who was she, and what was she to Jack?

From a distance, it seemed she had done the right thing in leaving, but there was always a niggling doubt. What if she had been wrong? Perhaps he could have explained. What if she had stayed? Would he have confided in her, told her the truth. She didn't know and she couldn't ask.

Cassie spent the rest of the day with a feeling of isolation. The thrilling trip of a lifetime had become as desolate as the landscape. She had to force herself to smile at people. She checked the papers for news.

Cassie's two older brothers had moved out of home, but called the motel and gave their opinions on her options for returning home. America was a lifetime away but it seemed that everything was going along as usual. She longed to be back hunting for fossils. At least they never tried to tell her what to do, or rearrange her life. They didn't lie or cheat or pretend. They were dead, and couldn't cause pain to anyone.

Knowing it would be a long time before she could return to Australia once she went home, Cassie decided to disregard her families pleas and stand firm on her determination to go to Alcoota. She would join the dig, single-handedly make an astonishing discovery and become an internationally acclaimed dinosaur expert.

Then she could forget about Jack.

Nine

The following day, Cassie was searching for her professor's tattered letter of introduction in her shoulder bag, and came across the papers she had forgotten to replace in Jack's SUV. It was a blow to her heart. All she'd felt for Jack came flooding back, the good feelings and the pain of betrayal.

She knew then that she had only been pretending it was over. After thinking seriously about how much she missed him, she decided to look up his telephone number, in case he'd gone back to Melbourne. After all, she thought, it would be a few weeks before that damn hybrid poppy would be ready for Silverton to collect, and he does have an office down there. I might as well find out if he is okay. He can only tell me to get lost.

She hesitated when she found the number, but she thought, damn it, what can I lose, and dialed. A woman said, "Hello."

Cassie was shocked. She thought, maybe he's married. Maybe that woman in Jasper Creek was his wife, or his girlfriend. That would be the last straw in a whole bale of rotten hay.

The woman continued sharply, "Elise Blackwood here, who's calling please?"

"Hello, Mrs. Blackwood. Could I speak to Jack?" Cassie thought for a moment nerves would shut her voice down. That must be his mother. Cassie felt a sense of relief.

"Who is this?"

"My name is Cassie Travis. I met Jack here in the Northern Territory."

There was a flicker of hesitation, then, "Look, Cassie, I'm sorry. If you're a friend of Jack, I have to tell you, he's not back from the desert. We don't know where he is." Her voice was cultured but with an overtone of distress. "He said he'd call, but he didn't, and he doesn't answer his cell phone. His father and I are very worried about his safety."

"I'm sorry to hear Jack is missing." Battling a cloud of foreboding, Cassie took a deep breath, determined not to break down. "Is there anything I can do?"

There was silence for a moment, then, "Perhaps you could give us some clue as to his whereabouts?"

Mrs. Blackwood's concern was palpable, leaving Cassie confused and worried. All she could think was how she'd left Jack, and now he was missing. She'd allowed her rotten temper to get the upper hand and had stolen his SUV, leaving him without a vehicle. The horses weren't much good for long treks. They'd been pretty much flogged by Blue and Kev and their hooves badly needed attention.

Surely the police would have checked on Jack? No, they were keeping well out of the picture until Silverton returned to Jasper Creek to collect his poppy plants.

So it probably *was* her fault he hadn't gone home. Cassie sighed. His parents would never forgive her and she couldn't blame them. Then she remembered seeing him in Jasper Creek with that woman and was even more confused. Surely he was safe then? Maybe Silverton and his men had come back early to steal the research, and somehow discovered there was a trap being set. Jack was only one man, strong and resourceful, but could he fight five men with guns and win? Not likely.

Now she was talking to Jack's mother and she seemed like such a lovely lady. She was confiding in Cassie, seeking her counsel like she was Jack's long lost friend rather than the one who had caused their son to disappear. Cassie felt so guilty about her part that she could hardly speak.

She decided to tell his parents what she had done, she referred to him as Jason, but his mother said, "He thought Jason was a sissy name when he was eight and asked us to call him Jack." She laughed. "He was taking charge even then."

Cassie laughed too. She knew what Mrs. Blackwood meant. "Yes, that's Jack."

After she told her story they, both Jack's parents, very kindly, and generously in the circumstances, set her mind at ease. His father came on the line and said, "Jack called us when he arrived in Jasper Creek the day after you'd gone. As well as the SUV, he has a motorcycle, so he wasn't stranded. He told us about you. He was fine then, Cassie. I think he wasn't too happy you'd gone, though. He seemed to think you were friends and couldn't understand why you left."

"So he told you about me?"

"He certainly did. Said he was just getting to know you, and suddenly you were gone. It was quite a surprise to us that he talked about a girl. He usually keeps things like that to himself."

She broke down then and told them the rest of the story, only leaving out the part about her suspicions. They were a kind couple and she didn't want to cause them unnecessary pain. When she had completed the process of unburdening herself and the kindly words of reassurance subsided, Mr. Blackwood said, "We could let you know when Jack calls. We've got a friend in the area who is keeping an eye out for him."

Cassie said, "Who is it? I might know them."

Mr. Blackwood said, "Alicia McFarlane. She owns the Jasper Creek Hotel."

Cassie gasped. "Is she a tall, blonde woman? Looks like a model?"

"That's her. Nice woman. Very efficient. If anyone can find Jack, it'll be Alicia. She has a nose like a bloodhound."

Cassie had the uncharitable wish that Alicia's nose really was like a bloodhound. Then Jack might not be quite so keen to sit in the hotel, drinking with her. She'd have to stay outside, in a kennel. Cassie smiled. What a lovely thought. She'd be happy to find some old bones for her to chew on.

Seemingly sensing her consternation when coming on the line to say her farewells, Mrs. Blackwood spoke to Cassie in a kindly voice. "We don't know much about what's going on up there. Jack keeps things to himself. Doesn't want to worry us. We only know he collects plants for research. He told us everything else is confidential. That's the rule with the people he works for. Secrecy is what they live for."

Later that night, Cassie made a decision. She didn't want to miss out on going to Alcoota when she was this close. New discoveries were being made, and she was missing out on the action. She could hire a car in Alice Springs. With careful planning, and extra supplies, she could visit Morialta Gorge on the way, just to see if Jack was okay. No big deal. Call in, say hi, and then head on up to Alcoota. She'd call his parents from Jasper Creek on her way back through.

Apologizing for leaving the way she did would be hard. Cassie wasn't comfortable admitting she was wrong. He may not forgive her, but she had to try. She just prayed it wasn't too late. Maybe he could come to Alcoota with her? She'd love to share with him the pleasure of bringing pieces of an ancient world into the light of day. He could look for botanical specimens, and she could dig bones out of the ground. It would be fun.

Cassie headed away from Alice Springs into the East MacDonnell ranges, negotiating the single lane Plenty Highway before taking a turn off to the left. There were supposed to be cattle stations in the region, but they were so vast, it was an endless journey to find a homestead. She had hired an SUV the same as Jack's, but dark blue in color — no chance of a break down this time!

The land was covered with coarse red sand, bushes and stubbly trees. Hills and large rock formations gave it an untamed quality. River Red Gums grew along sandy riverbeds, their roots buried far underground. In late October, it was a land waiting for rain; floods had passed and the water they'd seen had already soaked into the ground.

She hoped it wouldn't rain while she was there, Alcoota wasn't so bad, but this area was threaded with dry creeks, and prone to flash floods. The advice she'd had was, 'if it rains, get out immediately'. As she drove, she reflected on her reasons for coming here. Jack didn't expect her. He probably thought she was in a library, stamping books. If he thought of her at all? She really ought to be making her way north to Alcoota. Two weeks wasn't much time to spend at the fossil beds. Calling in on Jack was just indulging a fantasy.

She and Jack had never exchanged promises to each other, or vows. They had made love, but knew each in other ways, ways that were subliminal, but deep all the same.

Surely she would have known if he was accepting money from Silverton? The whole thing didn't make sense any more. Maybe she had totally over-reacted to hearing him talk about that bank account? Trouble was, she wasn't a mind reader. He wouldn't stay to answer her questions, and the evidence of her own ears was damning.

Well, now it was her turn to show she could care for him, even if he didn't want it. He probably felt they were wrong for each other, but she wanted to show him that didn't matter, so long as they loved each other. Then again, maybe he didn't love her? He'd never said he did, just held her in his arms and made her believe it. Maybe she was dreaming, again?

The closer Cassie got to Morialta Gorge, the more she felt that something was wrong. It was a long drive, and she had time to think about the situation. Gut instinct told her he was not the type of man to worry his parents. What could have happened after his phone call home? Soon she would be at the camp and she would see for herself.

She'd made sure there was a CB radio in the vehicle for her to contact the flying doctor, or police if necessary. She fervently hoped that would not be the case. She had read about the Flying Doctor Service in Australia. It was similar to AeroCare in America. Not that she'd ever needed to use their services, but she knew they were there. Trouble was, a cell phone was necessary to contact them.

It had been days since she left him, and since she'd spoken to Jack's parents, Cassie had drawn out all her savings, incurring the wrath of her parents. She'd ignored their request to catch a plane back to America and let the Australian authorities handle the situation.

The Travis's had been shocked when she told them some of what had happened. They felt it was like the old west, people with guns and drug running. She told them the police were staying out of the area for the moment.

Police told the Blackwood family that Jack had contacted them a week ago. But Cassie was uneasy. His parents had talked about a motorcycle, which, everyone knew, was dangerous, unreliable in sand. She just wanted to see if he was okay.

Driving along the narrow road leading to the gorge, Cassie looked for the entrance to the track. Finding it proved very difficult, but after climbing out of the SUV and searching on foot, Cassie eventually located the red cloth she had tied to a tree. She turned the vehicle onto the overgrown track, crushing bushes as she went. It appeared to have had little traffic since she had last been there.

At last, after traveling slowly along the winding track for about half an hour, Cassie arrived at the cave. She parked, and looked around. Jack wasn't there, but the sight of his white SUV standing outside the cave was a welcome sight. It was unlocked, so Cassie put his license and papers in the glove compartment.

Wondering if he'd even noticed they were gone; she walked along the path by the river, through the rocky entrance to the gorge.

Her heart lurched at the familiarity of her surroundings. She felt she had come home. "Jack! Are you there?" she called as she reached the camp, searching apprehensively for the man she had wanted and needed for so long.

There was silence. Time stopped for Cassie as she came to terms with Jack's absence. Her world was poised on a knife edge. All it would take to slice her to ribbons was her acceptance of pain. She was still alone. Then, a moment later, anger started to ferment inside her. How could he leave her like this? After what they had been through, all the time they had spent working on understanding each other was for nothing. How could you talk to someone who wasn't there? If Cassie had still held Jack's papers at that moment, she would have hurled them into the river.

She turned sharply as a mocking voice came from under a tree, "So, you're back?"

Cassie's face lit up with joy. "Jack! You're here!" She wanted to hurl herself into his arms and hug him, she was so pleased to see him alive, and in almost one piece. At the same moment, she wanted to teach him a lesson. Hitting him over the head with something solid was her next idea. Maybe he'd remember the pain next time he let her down. She barely had time to notice the bandage on his leg, and the fact that he made no move toward her, when the expression on his face stopped her cold. He was hostile and definitely unwelcoming.

She knew he would be angry she had borrowed his SUV but hoped he would have forgiven her by now? After all, he hadn't spoken harshly about her to his parents. Maybe they had held something back, not wanting to upset her.

The apology she had planned to make was hovering on her tongue when he said, "I'm here, Cassie. The question is, what are you doing here?"

"Well," she said slowly, her apology stillborn, "I was on my way to Alcoota, and so I called in to see if you were okay. Your parents are worried, you didn't call them when you said you would." She stepped back involuntarily when he glared at her, tripping over the poles holding up the shelter, falling on her rear end in the dirt.

She sat at his feet, rubbing her sore spots and scowling up at Jack as if he were responsible for her undignified fall. This wasn't how she'd intended this meeting to go.

She had come to talk, openly and honestly. She hoped he would feel the same, hopefully welcoming her back. It looked like he needed her help as well, but it seemed she was a little premature in her assumptions. His arms were not open to her.

I may as well go straight to Alcoota and commune with dinosaurs, she thought. I'll get a warmer welcome from them, and they won't glare accusingly.

Cassie stood up, dusting herself off. Jack hobbled over to a tree stump and sat down. "So, you spoke to my parents," he said. "I suppose they gave you the royal treatment, polite reassurance that you're not to blame?"

"*Some* people are civilized, Jack." Cassie felt vulnerable within but tried not to show it. "Why are you acting like this? You got your SUV back so you can't still be mad at me. You were gone, and I had to get on with my life."

Her softly pleading brown eyes distracted him for a moment, but then he hardened his heart against her sweet face and his reluctantly softened inclinations. "I'm a little confused Cassie. First of all, you take my SUV, and then you dump it in a side street in Jasper Creek without telling anyone. I suppose I'm lucky you saw fit to leave the keys under the seat. I only found it by chance when I walked around to the garage workshop in the side street. Imagine my surprise when I found my car sitting on the side of the road. Anyone could have taken it."

Cassie couldn't speak. How to refute the truth was beyond her.

He scowled at her. "And, as if that wasn't enough, you turn up here, out of the blue, expecting me to welcome you back." He sighed and shook his head, "Cassie, you stole my SUV. I should call the police and have you arrested!"

"You can't. I gave it back."

"So you did. How considerate of you."

"Wasn't it? So, now that I'm here, tell me what's going on. I heard some things before I left. In fact, that's one of the reasons I left. I went for a walk over the hill. I heard you talking to some men. I heard the name Silverton and I knew who it was."

"So that was you? I thought it was a galah in the trees."

"That's that pink bird isn't it. Big and noisy. Very funny, Jack. I heard you say, 'put the money in my bank account'. I was shocked. I thought you were working with the police to catch Silverton, not get money from him."

Jack groaned. "I didn't know you were listening. I don't need money. It was part of the deal. The police told me to ask for the money to be paid in advance. Silverton would believe that was normal behavior for a man willing to sell out his company."

"I didn't even know where you were going. You should have told me what you were going to do," she accused. "Didn't you trust me to keep my mouth shut?"

"I would have told you, if I thought you would be eavesdropping. That's a nasty little habit you've got there, Cassie Travis."

"I like to know what's going on. Tell me, why didn't we camp at the field lab?"

"There's nothing much there, just a cave with equipment. Nothing else. This is much nicer, and you can swim here."

"You left me alone, in a strange country, to fend for myself. After all that happened, you just walked away. No explanation."

Jack didn't answer. What could he say? 'I went away to save you' was only part of the truth.

Cassie glared at Jack as he stood, silent as the grave,

his communication skills at an all time low. She said, "If you told me about the radio and the SUV hidden away I would have felt much more confident. I could have saved myself, if necessary."

When he turned away and looked out over the trees, she said, her voice quiet and full of pain, "If you trusted me, I could even have saved you."

Shrugging his shoulders, not looking at Cassie, his hard and uncompromising tone swept across her defenses. "I didn't need saving."

He was reluctant to talk about trust. It had been a long time since he had trusted anybody. The world he inhabited was built on deception and he had become part of that mindset. It was inside his subconscious, so deep that he didn't know if it would ever leave him.

She indicated his bandaged leg. "So, what's this all about?"

Jack shrugged as if it were nothing. "I had an accident on my motor-bike. I ran into some trouble, it flipped and fell on top of me. It's getting better. In a couple of weeks I'll be mobile again."

He was treating himself by rubbing the wound with a saltbush plant but it didn't seem to be working. Antibiotics were unattainable without a pharmacy. His first-aid kit had somehow been woefully ill equipped for a man in his line of work. He didn't want to admit that to Cassie. She had enough ammunition against him already.

"So, what was the trouble you had with the bike?"

He picked up a makeshift crutch, stood on his good leg and limped to the campfire where a pot of water was boiling.

After he had thrown a handful of tea in and removed the pot from the fire with a stick he said, "I was going too fast. The tires spun out in the dust." He grinned maliciously up at her. "You can take the blame for that Cassie. I was feeling like throttling you, and not concentrating on what I was doing. Would you like a cup?"

Ignoring his offer, she refused to feel guilty, "Okay, so it's my fault you're a lousy rider. You have to blame somebody so why not me. How bad is it?"

"Could be worse." Jack stifled a groan of pain. The wound under his foot was becoming swollen and red. He couldn't see it clearly but he knew it needed medical treatment. His boots had been totally wrecked, and so had the bike.

"Not much worse," commented Cassie dryly. "Why haven't you called the flying doctor? I've heard they go all over Australia and pick up anybody, anywhere."

"I'm only able to move around the camp a little bit. It's hell to put pressure on my foot. I've been waiting to see if it improved before attempting to get to the cave where I could radio for help."

"You didn't make it, did you? You look like you've got a fever."

He looked at her grimly, feeling perspiration gather. "Tell me about it. I put my back out as well and that made it even more difficult to go anywhere."

Cassie put her hand out to touch his forehead. It was hot. She said, "You'd better get back under the shade. I'll get some water to cool you down."

When she came back with water, she bathed his face, looking sternly at him as she said, "This has gone on too long, Jack. You need help. I'll call the flying doctor for you."

"Look, I know I need help. Don't rub it in. I was trying to fix it with natural remedies but it isn't working."

"Figures. I saw you, you know. In Jasper Creek that day."

"Where did you see me?" He tried to get up but subsided with a groan of pain. He said fiercely, rubbing his back, "Tell me what happened."

"I was with a truck driver across the road. He was giving me a ride to Alice Springs. You were with a woman. Drinking in the pub." A small flame of jealousy needled Cassie as she asked the question. "What were you doing with her?"

Jack saw the flame and was satisfied. His red-haired torment had given him hell for long enough, and now it was his turn to give her a taste of her own medicine. "We were having lunch. She's good company, very accommodating. She'll do anything for me."

"I bet she will." Cassie gritted, unable to control her resentment. "Your mother told me about her. She said her name is Alicia McFarlane."

"Yeah. She's a widow. The pub belongs to her. She runs it herself. Very efficiently. The food there is good too." He allowed himself a small grin. "A man could do a lot worse than take up with her. She doesn't irritate me. She's easy on the eye. She dresses well. She's intelligent. She's got money to burn. Add to that a large slice of sex appeal, I reckon you've got a winner."

He sighed and looked off into the distance as if entranced at the thought of the luscious Alicia, available rich widow. Out of the corner of his eye he saw red in Cassie's cheeks. Maybe she had a fever too. She looked like she wanted to kill someone. Probably him. Her hands were clenched and her back rigid, her lips tight.

"Well," she said stiffly, "I hope you'll be very happy. When is the big day or haven't you got around to working it out yet? Too busy being accommodated I suppose?"

"I have to admit we've been a little too busy to discuss anything like that." He smiled as if in memory of their activities. If only she knew. Alicia was accommodating several under-cover police officers at her hotel. She was far too busy to bother with anything else. He said, "She's got a lot of energy. I like that in a woman."

"You like that do you? Better make sure you can keep up with her," she said cuttingly. "Does the perfect Alicia know what you do out here in the outback?"

"She knows about my research."

"Ah, but does she know you live in squalor and shoot pigs to eat?"

"She knows all she needs to know. Anyway, I don't think she minds what I do."

"How wonderful for both of you. I can see I spent a wasted trip coming out here. No doubt you're waiting for her to come for you. I'll tell your parents you'll be in touch shall I? Better still, you can call them yourself. They might like to hear your voice."

Jack groaned. Talking to his parents was the last thing he wanted to do. They'd ask questions, and his answers were thin on the ground.

Cassie nodded. "I can see you're in too much pain to get to the cave. I better get this show on the road."

Jack grinned. She was so mad, she'd do anything.

Cassie turned toward the path along the river without commenting. What's the use she thought? He's already made plans for his life and I'm not part of them. I'll go before I give myself away and slap that satisfied grin off his face.

When she returned, the satisfied grin on her face told him she was back in control of her emotions. Then she turned and walked along the river path. "I'll just look and see if the plane is coming. I should be able to see it from the ridge.

Jack, realizing she was leaving, knew that he'd better do something, fast. He let out a groan of pain and lowered himself flat on the ground.

Cassie turned back, saying, "Oh, hell, I suppose I'd better give you a hand. Your mother is such a nice lady. How she had a son like you I'll never know."

"I'll probably live. Don't put yourself out, Cassie." Jack hated feeling sorry for himself. It seemed to be happening quite a lot lately. Maybe he needed some distance from his problem. The Flying Doctor coming would be the perfect excuse.

"I won't." All thought of leaving was gone, for the moment. She had radioed the flying doctor, now Jack would get to a hospital where his leg could be treated. He wouldn't need her any more, so she should be grateful. She wasn't.

"Hang on while I check on the plane."

Jack didn't protest. There would be time enough later for him to explain about Alicia.

I could always introduce them, let her see that we're just friends, he thought. Then he chided himself for being delusional. It would take more than an introduction and a tea party to get back on Cassie's good side. It would take a miracle.

Jack was certain he had never been in so much bother in his life until he met Cassie Travis. He conceded he might have been a little hasty in letting her believe those things about himself and Alicia but, damn it, she deserved to be on hot coals for a while.

That is, if she was on hot coals? He felt his confidence waiver, a debilitating thing for a man who ran his own successful business. Maybe she had no interest in him after all? He was no expert with women. Could he have read her wrong? If he had, could he blame it on the fever?

Delirium perhaps? He did have a red face and sweaty palms. It was time to sort this thing out once and for all? Then he'd know how she felt.

When she came back he said, "Cassie, about Alicia. I think I'd better explain a few things. Clear the air, you know how it is?"

"Not necessary." Cassie cut him off before he could say any more. "I know how you feel, Jack. No need to go into it now. The flying doctor will be landing out next to the road. Probably an hour or so. I'm not sure. I've given them directions, but I'll lay down a signal in the open area near the entrance to the track into here."

"What kind of signal?"

"I can use a couple of white shirts, spread them out on a flat area."

"They should be able to see that," said Jack. "Cassie, I wish you'd sit still and let me tell you…"

Once again she kept talking and refused to look at him. The wall she had built was rock solid. "It would be best if we drive out there now?" she said. Jack groaned.

"That way they won't miss us," she continued. "The sooner you get yourself attended to the quicker I can get to Alcoota. I've got a lot to do up there. They're expecting me."

Cassie smiled maliciously. "There's someone waiting for me in Nevada too. Someone special." She didn't say who it was. She didn't mention the elderly professor who was her paleontology mentor. Jack would probably die laughing. So would the professor.

"But Cassie. Wait a minute. Stop for a second and hear me out." What was she talking about? Someone special! Who the hell could she have waiting for her? The guy had to be an idiot, letting her take off into the wilderness to find another man. What a fool. "Who have you got waiting for you?" he snarled.

"No-one you need to think about." Cassie tried to think of someone she could talk about. There was only professor Wilson who came to mind.

Jack wondered why Cassie was looking anywhere but at him. Maybe she'd invented someone waiting for her back home in the States? Maybe he'd driven her to it?

"Look, that situation with Alicia, it's not what you think."

"I think it's exactly what I think. I saw her, remember. You were all over her."

"I hardly touched her." Jack protested. "I only stayed in the hotel, not with Alicia. She was too busy with the police…" He suddenly realized the hole he had dug for himself. It was deep.

Cassie's smile was faintly malicious. "If you don't mind, I'd prefer to drop the subject. I don't wish to discuss your free room and board any longer. If you've got anything to take with you, tell me now. I'll get your stuff."

Resigned for the moment, Jack said, "Just my pack. It's in the tent."

When she came back with his pack, he stood up and she took his arm. "Come on, I'll help you." As she touched his firm brown skin, she reminded herself he was just a man, not an irresistible force of nature.

So why did her palm tingle, her flesh yearn? She wished there was a switch; she would turn it off before she burst into flames.

Together they slowly made their way down the river path, through the rocks and into the area in front of the cave. It seemed to take forever.

Jack said, "Wait a minute. I want to get something else." He hobbled into the cave, using his stick, coming back with a bag. "My research. Can't leave this behind."

"Is that all you want?" she asked.

"That's all," he replied, back to being the silent, indomitable male. What was the point of talking? Cassie wouldn't listen to anything he had to say, not now.

On the way out to the main road in her SUV, she was silent, leaving a frustrated Jack to ponder his own actions and words. He was not very happy with his conclusions, and her accusations walked around in his brain like a destructive laser beam.

What was he going to do, he wondered in despair? She refused to listen to him. It was no comfort knowing he had spoken about Alicia in more than glowing terms, thereby forcing Cassie to consider him intimately involved with the woman. If his foot didn't hurt so much, he'd kick himself.

Alicia would be horrified at such innuendo about her; she had a long-standing relationship with a highly respected station owner in the district. She was also a friend of his mother. If she and Cassie compared notes, they would both be after his blood.

He reflected grimly that they would have to stand in line. The crash that had caused him to become separated from his motorbike was not an accident.

As Cassie drove along the bush track, Jack had time to think about things, about Cassie and their involvement, and how he really felt. He realized he wanted to fight for Cassie and protect her. He loved her and as soon as he could tie her down to listen he would tell her so. Then it would be up to her.

Jack said, "Thank you for coming to look for me, Cassie. I might snarl at you, but I am grateful."

"So, tell me how the accident really happened?" Cassie had on what Jack referred to as her stubborn look. She was like a terrier gripping a rat. He knew when to give in and retain some dignity. "Don't leave anything out," she ordered. "I'll know."

"I rode my bike out to the main road to meet one of the undercover police. He must have got lost. Easy to do out here. On my way to Jasper Creek to find him, I came across Blue and Kev. They were real happy to see me, and decided to give me a memento of our friendship. I decided I wasn't ready for the gift they had in mind so I got on my bike and took off."

"I'd like to give them something," she growled.

Jack nodded. "Yeah. Me too. They followed me in their truck until the first bend in the road, so I decided to follow a track to the north. I planned to disappear into the hills. It's pretty rough country up there; I thought I'd lose them. I didn't even get to turn the corner. They came up behind me, ramming the bike, running me off into a shallow ravine at the side of the road."

"That sounds like them," she said. "Sneak up, strike while you're not looking. Bastards. I'd like to sneak up and show them a thing or two. They'd beg to be put out of their misery before I finished."

"I'd like to see that." Jack laughed. At least she was now on his side. "Anyway, I put my foot down to stop, caught my boot on something sharp, the bike flew up in the air, then fell on top of me. Hurt like hell too. The last I saw was their truck taking off down the road leaving me for dead."

"I wonder if they attacked you because Silverton told them to?"

"I think this was on their own. Silverton doesn't want me dead, not yet. He wants those plants and the research verified. And he wants me to keep quiet about him. After he's satisfied, who knows? Silverton went back to Alice Springs after he came to the compound that day. He's not due back until the plants are mature. I'm supposed to let him know."

"How do you get into so much trouble, Jack?"

"Just luck and good management I guess."

"No, I think you've got a death wish."

Jack shrugged. "Yeah, I think I do. I picked you up, didn't I?"

She thumped his arm, he groaned in pain. "I already had a bruise on that arm."

Cassie laughed. "Now you've got another one." She rubbed the spot on his arm without slowing down. At least they were communicating again. It was a start.

Ten

The flying doctor's airplane touched down in the field with hardly a bounce. Cassie was impressed with the way the doctor and nurse took charge of Jack. She hardly had time to say goodbye before they were turning to taxi down the road, leaving her alone with her thoughts. She had a long drive ahead of her, now was not the time to start brooding about something that was out of her hands.

After she arrived at Alice Springs, Cassie called the flying doctor service and asked where Jack had been taken. When she was told there was only one hospital in Alice Springs and been given the address and phone number, she found herself a room at a motel.

She picked up the telephone early the next day. "Mrs. Blackwood? This is Cassie Travis. I wanted to tell you myself, I found Jack."

"Cassie, how lovely to hear from you. Jack called us last night to tell us what happened. Thank you very much for what you did. His father and I are so relieved. Maybe a short stay in hospital will keep him out of trouble for a while. At least I won't worry while he's there being looked after. He said his foot was infected. Nothing to worry about."

Trust Jack to play down his injury. It was more than infected, there was a red streak going up his ankle. Cassie didn't think he would have told his parents how the accident happened, and she didn't want to worry them.

"We'd come up and see him, only he said he'd be out of there soon."

"Yes, I'm sure he will. I'll keep an eye on him, Mrs. Blackwood. Don't worry."

"He'll be grouchy for a while." Cassie had to agree.

Mrs. Blackwood sighed. "He gets a bit impatient with medical procedures. He was in hospital having his appendix out a few years ago. He was very naughty. Gave the nurses hell. He wanted to discharge himself before his doctor said he was ready."

Cassie laughed. "That sounds like him. Did he want to take out his own stitches?"

Mrs. Blackwood chuckled. "Yes, he did. Of course they refused. This time will be worse. He's not really sick enough to stay in bed. He won't be happy, but he doesn't get aggressive, he just broods, and snarls a bit. He feels caged. Like a tiger."

"I know what you mean." Cassie smiled. "He gets a bit primal when he's irritated."

"That's it, dear. Primal. You've got it exactly. I'm so glad you understand and forgive him for it. Not everyone does you know, especially women. They expect him to be all sweetness and light when he feels as black as thunder. He has a really effective scowl. You might have seen it. Water off a duck's back if you understand him. His father's the same. A man of great passion."

"Yes, I do understand him, Mrs. Blackwood," Cassie said softly. "We got to know each other quite well. I have to go now. I'll talk to you later. And thanks."

Cassie rang off, planning to see Jack. She didn't think he was going to be out of the hospital as fast as he hoped. She unpacked her things and took a shower. She wanted to be ready early in the afternoon to go to the hospital. Then, after deciding what jeans and shirt to wear, she called her parents.

Cassie's mother said, "It's time you stopped those

treks into the wilderness, Cassie. I've heard that it's hard country over there in Australia."

"I'm getting tougher, Mom. I really like it here. It's a bit like Nevada."

"When are you coming home?"

Cassie was busy putting face cream on as she talked, trying to counteract the ravages of too much sun. "I can't come back until I've been to Alcoota. It's what I came to Australia for. I want to see something of life."

"Prehistoric bones aren't life, Cassie. They're dead. Getting married and having babies is life."

"Later, maybe."

Cassie could hear her mother sigh on the phone. There was a lecture coming. She could hear it. If she was quick, she could head it off at the pass.

"Mom, I've met most of your friends sons. They bore me to tears. Half of them still live at home and ask their mothers for permission to date. I want a man who knows what a woman wants. And if he doesn't know he should have enough intelligence to ask. Those guys would be afraid of the answers they'd get. So, no, I'm not coming back. Not just yet. Sorry."

Cassie's mother was too much of a lady to lose her temper but her tone was like broken glass. "You don't sound sorry. Is anyone expecting you at Alcoota?"

"I have a letter of introduction. I have to go now. I'm visiting a friend in hospital."

"Oh. That's kind of you." Her mother warmed up a little. "Nothing serious, I hope."

"No. A sore foot, nothing serious." Cassie didn't say it was a man, she'd never hear the end of it. "It's just someone I met recently."

"Well, you need to meet new people."

Cassie could hear a lecture coming on, and knew it

was time to hang up. She didn't want to make her mother unhappy, but she had to live her own life. "Mom, I have to go now. Give Dad my love. I'll call you."

Cassie understood her mother's need to see her children secure. She wanted her daughter to be safely married, living close by so she could see her grandchildren. But Cassie had not found her ideal man in Nevada, New York or even Nebraska. She had found him in outback Australia, walking on a bush track, carrying a rifle and looking like a hobo. Life could be so unexpected, and exciting. You just had to take a chance.

When she reached Jack's hospital room, Cassie hovered in the corridor for a few minutes, trying to calm her butterflies, and control her shaking hands. Anyone would think he was an ogre, the way she was behaving. Finally, she gripped her purse tightly and opened the door, holding a gift for him like a weapon.

There was a woman with him, a tall dark-haired woman, young, slim and beautiful. A gasp from Cassie brought their two heads around. The woman smiled at her. Jack scowled. "Cassie! Come in and shut the door."

Seeing that Cassie was tongue-tied, the woman said, "You must be the girl I've been hearing so much about." At Cassie's surprised look she continued. "Oh, not from Jack, from our mother. My brother is unable to string two polite words together at the moment. I think he's under the impression that if he growls enough they'll let him go home. Poor thing doesn't realize. They enjoy having him in their power. I'm Ronnie. Nice to meet you, Cassie."

"Nice to meet you too." Cassie smiled at Jack's sister.

Ronnie grinned, her hazel eyes twinkling with merriment. "I think they've got him scheduled for a sponge bath later. I'd love to be a fly on the wall."

"Shut up, Ronnie!" Jack growled. "Your mouth will get you into big trouble one of these days."

Cassie took that moment to look at Jack properly. The beard was gone and he looked a different person, younger, slightly less aggressive. Then he opened his mouth and it was the old Jack who spoke. She felt reassured, even as she was angered by his words.

"What are you doing here, Cassie?" Having time to think hadn't improved Jack's temper. He knew he was on edge, but his foot was on fire, as well as itching like crazy. He wanted to get out for some fresh air. He hated hospitals, especially on this side of the blankets.

Cassie glared, refusing to allow the deep hurt from his rejection to show. "I had the idea you might be glad to have a visitor. Silly me. I'll go back to the motel."

Cassie dumped a box unceremoniously on his lap, and he scowled, even while he unwrapped it. He took a chocolate and bit into it. She almost smiled at the way he tasted the sweet treat, licking his lips with evident enjoyment. Ronnie watched him too, smiling, and the two girls shared a moment of understanding. It was short-lived.

"I wouldn't get any more ideas if I were you, Cassie. They usually land you in trouble. Why don't you go home to America? That way you'll be safe." And out of my hair was unsaid, but understood.

Ronnie turned to her brother. "There's no need to speak like that. Cassie took the time to come here to see you, so the least you could do is be polite. It's not like you to be so rude to people. What would Mother and Dad say?"

"It is like me to be rude to people." Jack put aside the half empty box of chocolates, wiping his hands on a tissue.

"He's right. He is rude." Cassie looked at Jack, lying in

the bed with his foot elevated, a hospital gown barely covering the essentials. She wanted to do something violent to him but was prevented by her surroundings. "I thought you'd be pleased to see me, but I was wrong. The only person you're pleased to see is yourself when you look in the mirror.

"It wasn't my intention to hurt you," Jack muttered, looking uncomfortable.

"Too late. You've already done it." Cassie's voice vibrated. "Let me tell you, Jack, you're not that interesting. Your manners are atrocious, you're nasty, you're pig-headed and I have no intention of coming here ever again. How a primitive creature like you managed to have such a nice family is a miracle. Maybe you're a throwback."

"I'd *like* to throw him back," put in Ronnie, laughing. She was ignored, so she sat on the bed, and watched. It was like a tennis match, look one way, and then the other, no impact, but this was definitely a contest.

"Ronnie," warned Jack, not looking at his sister. "I didn't mean to hurt you, Cassie. You really would be better off away from here."

"It's too late to start crawling back into my good books. They're closed. And don't tell me what to do. You've got no right to tell me to do anything." Cassie turned and yanked the door open. "And another thing," she said, turning back for a moment, "I hope those nurses give you hell. Every embarrassing treatment they can think up should be yours. Enemas. The lot. You deserve it! And while you're at it, get some pajamas. That gown is barely decent. You're falling out of it."

If it had been possible to slam the door, it would have been parted from its hinges, so great was the force of Cassie's indignation as she whirled through it. Instead, like most hospital doors, it closed quietly, and left behind a vacuum.

Jack looked down, wondering what was hanging out. Nothing vital was in view, thank goodness. Ronnie looked stunned, as if she had never seen such an eruption in her life before. "That's amazing. I thought tempers like that only raged in our family." She grinned. "You've done it now, Jack. You've finally met your match."

"She's gone now. There's nothing between us any more." Jack had the grace to feel embarrassed at the lie. He looked as if his only hope of redemption had just gone out the door.

"That's what you think," said Ronnie. She shook her head.

"It's what I know. It's finished, what there was of it. Just leave it alone. And don't tell the parents. They'll say it's my fault she left, I'll never hear the end of it."

"It *is* your fault. You were very rude Jack. I don't blame Cassie for being cross."

"That wasn't cross, that was Mt. Vesuvius erupting. Run for your life or you'll be swept away in hot lava."

Ronnie wondered at the smile he gave when he said that, but she knew it would be wiser not to ask.

For a moment she envied Cassie. She wished a man would think about her with such passion on his mind. She saw her brother as she had never seen him before, and knew that it was Cassie that made the difference. She hoped he would be smart enough to go after her when he was able. And when Jack found Cassie, Ronnie hoped she would listen and forgive.

"She's a beautiful girl." Ronnie prompted her brother. "She looks good in blue jeans. They fit her like a glove."

"She did look good didn't she? I've never seen her dressed, ah, dressed like that before. Ratty shorts or baggy t-shirts are her usual gear."

Ronnie thought he sounded disappointed. She grinned. Things were looking up.

"She must have cared a lot to come here, Jack. Why don't you give her a call?"

"I can't."

"Why not? It wouldn't kill you just to talk. I think you really hurt her tonight."

"She's better off without me, Ronnie."

"Playing God again, Jack? Why not let the girl decide for herself? If you care about her, tell her the truth and allow her to choose."

He didn't answer. Ronnie knew that brooding look, so she said, "Maybe she won't listen. She may have decided you're a dead loss. Personally, I'd tell you to get lost. But then, I'm not in love with you. I'm just your sister."

He looked up sharply at that. "Of course she's not in love with me. I haven't given her any reason to love me. I'm all the things she said, and more. There's no way she could love me."

"I think you're underestimating yourself, Jack. You need to take a good look at Cassie. Watch her when she's with you. You might be surprised at what you see."

"I'll have to find her first."

"That should be easy. Call every motel in Alice Springs. Travis isn't all that common a name."

Jack looked so forlorn, and unlike her confident older brother, that Ronnie was touched. "Don't worry. She could come back to see you."

He shook his head. "No, she won't. She has a stubborn streak even wider than mine. I'll have to wait until this foot heals, then try again to find her. It's my own damn fault if she never wants to see me again."

An honest girl, Ronnie said, "Yes, it is your fault. No one ever said asking for forgiveness is easy. I can call the motels. It would give me something to do tomorrow while I wait for the bus back to Adelaide. It goes late in the afternoon. If I find out anything, I'll call you."

"Do it if you want to, but be careful. Don't let anyone listen in to your conversation. There are some nasty people out there who want to see me dead. If Cassie is with me, she could share the same fate."

"Don't worry, big brother. I'll be careful."

Ronnie headed to the door, saying, "I'll come back with some pajamas. That gown is barely decent. Stripes okay?" The last thing she saw was Jack, grinning, dismissing her with a rude hand signal. At least he hadn't totally lost his sense of humor.

That evening, Cassie called her mother, telling her she was going to Alcoota the next day. Her mother said, "I wish you would give up those outback jaunts, Cassie. You're starting to talk like one of those Aussie truck drivers."

Cassie grinned. "That's okay. I'll fit right in." Just thinking of the kindly truck driver, and his unprintable expressions, made her feel at home. She was even starting to understand Aussie slang.

"I've got someone for you to meet when you come home. My friend, Dulcie Hall, has a son. Martin. He's just the right age for you, twenty-five. He's studying law at NYU."

"I've already met Martin. He was at a party I went to last year. He's not such a prize." Cassie thought of all the things she did to get rid of Martin Hall, and sighed. Life was full of nasty little surprises and he was one of them.

She missed Jack already. Life was an empty silent room without the one you loved.

After Cassie hung up the phone, she began to pack, ready to head out early the next morning. Staying mad at

Jack for a couple of hours satisfied something dark in her psyche, but when the initial fury had eased, she knew it wasn't enough. The way he had rejected her was painful in the extreme, but she still loved him.

Cassie woke early, having spent a restless night, thinking of what might have been. She came out of her room and entered the reception area of the motel. The key was in her hand when she felt someone standing behind her.

She turned. "Ronnie," she breathed. "What are you doing here? " She looked behind Jack's sister, as if she expected someone else to be there. Ronnie was alone. Cassie's shoulders drooped. What had she expected? He was still in hospital.

Jack's sister seemed uncertain. "Hi, Cassie. I wanted to talk to you."

Cassie's heart began to beat a little faster. "Did Jack send you?"

"He wants to see you."

"Look, I was about to get some breakfast," said Cassie. "We can talk over coffee?"

"Sounds good."

When the two girls were seated in a modest cafe, they ordered breakfast. Ronnie said, "I just want to know how you feel about Jack?" At Cassie's uncertain look she continued. "He's my brother. I want him to be happy. I don't want to upset you. I tend to speak first, and then try to explain myself. It doesn't always work."

"It's okay, Ronnie. I understand. I think Jack and I both need time alone. Is his foot getting better? I didn't get a chance to ask."

"Yes. It's okay. He's on crutches. His main problem is being cooped up."

"Yes," said Cassie. "I know how that feels. I work in

the back room of a library. Jack needs to be patient. He's used to being on the move. Like me. I'm going north for a while, leaving today."

"Would you go to see him before you leave?"

"He wanted me to go away. As I recall he was quite rude."

"Yes, he was rude. Being pig headed is a family trait."

Cassie smiled slightly. "It's in my family too. I have a little trouble accepting males as the master race. I get into some wicked arguments with my brothers."

"I'm the same, I've never felt inferior. I've always known I was equal to anyone, even my big brother. He tried for years to convince me that I was his to command, especially when it came to doing dishes. Since he met you, he's changed. I think you've worked a miracle. Now he listens to my point of view."

"I wish he'd listen to mine. I thought he'd forgiven me for borrowing his SUV. I hoped we could start again, but I see now it's unrealistic."

"He misses you, Cassie. We talked after you left last night, and he told me why he told you to go. He was trying to protect you. Apparently he's involved in a police matter. Something to do with his drug research. Who would have thought Jasper Creek could be dangerous in that way? Anyway, he doesn't want you caught up in it."

"I'm already in it. I met some of the people he's dealing with." Cassie's voice took on a new strength. "I don't want him hurt either. He means a lot to me."

Ronnie grinned mischievously. "I know he does. It's funny. Sometimes his mind will be thinking one thing and his mouth saying another."

"I'm like that too," smiled Cassie. "It takes a while for your mouth to catch up."

"That's the trouble with clever people. They can hurt

you without meaning to, or wanting to, and quite often they hurt themselves too. You have to see past the words to catch the true meaning. Listen with your heart. It's worth doing if you care enough."

Cassie looked at Ronnie with hope in her eyes. "Are you saying he cares about me, Ronnie?" She looked suspicious suddenly. "He never said so."

"He will. He'll be out of there in a few days."

What would she do if she saw him? Jumping on him and dragging him into a bedroom was her action of choice, with a little one on one communication activity. But what if he didn't love her, or even like her a little? Would he use her for sex because there was no one else?

That idea fell through when she thought about Jack, how he looked, talked, made love. Any woman would want him, any time, any way, any where. He was every woman's dream.

And in the end, would he stay with her, or walk away without a second thought? Could she take that chance? If she did, and failed to keep him, would she survive?

"That's too late for me, Ronnie. I'm on my way as soon as I've finished my coffee."

"What about Jack?" Ronnie looked dismayed.

"I can't wait for him. I've got bones to look for at Alcoota. Tell him to call me when he's sorted himself out."

Ronnie sighed. "Better give me your cell phone number."

Alcoota was a dream come true. Clay pans, coarse red sand, rocks, dust and heat were part of it all. Cassie loved it. As an experienced participant, she was welcomed with open arms by the team already in residence. Their tents were spread out around the perimeter of the dig, giving a feeling of familiarity. Cassie was comfortable with tents, having spent much of her life camping. She was put to work immediately, after a cup of coffee, and didn't stop for a week, except to eat and sleep. She'd brought her own tent and supplies in Alice Springs in order to be self-sufficient.

A lot of the work was using a brush to carefully sweep dust off the bones that had been found already. They had to be photographed, mapped, and carefully extracted, to make way for possible future discoveries. Their exact location was recorded, before their preparation for transport to a museum.

It was slow work, tedious and painstaking. Mostly sorting unrecognizable, but possibly important, fossils, separating them from the pieces of rock and rubble embedded in the earth. Someone had brought a portable radio, so there was at least something to listen to, apart from the silence, and metal tools scraping rocks.

Wheelbarrows and large plastic buckets were used to cart the sand and rocks away. When the buckets were full, they were too heavy to lift, so Cassie had to ask for help. It was a companionable dig, everyone friendly, dedicated to their work, but when night came, and a camp fire was lit, stories of other digs and finds were told. There was a reverence for history in this place, with these people, that was an affirmation of Cassie's love of paleontology. She had only a short time, so she made the most of the experience. She tried to forget about Jack, and his concerns with the police operation and Gerald Silverton. Some of the time, she managed, but every now and then, when the camp bedded down for the night, and she was alone in her one-man tent, the breeze sighed through the trees, and she remembered how it had felt to be held in his arms. Waking suddenly each morning, just before daybreak, brought memories of him loving her, kissing her lips and of his gentle voice telling her how much he loved her. She could never believe it was real as the images in her mind vanished with the dawn. As soon as the sun came up, work would begin on the site in earnest. Just keeping exhaustion at bay was a full time job so there was no room for anything else.

Eleven

♡

Cassie left Alcoota with regret. She'd used her time well, learning from the experts, listening to their stories, absorbing the atmosphere of dedication. It was a long trip back to Alice Springs where she renewed her supplies, and called her mother. Everywhere she went she saw places she had been with Jack, and the memory of how he had loved her, and taken care of her, were hard to forget, returning again and again with renewed impact. How could she ever forget him? Forgiving him was something else again.

During the time in Alcoota, she had tried to forget Jack. It hadn't worked, so she knew it was time to make a decision. Did she want to see him? The answer was a definite yes, so she loaded up her SUV and headed to Morialta Gorge.

Jack could disappear for weeks at a time, as she well knew. There was a good chance she'd find him in Jasper Creek, but if he was with Alicia McFarlane, Cassie didn't know what she would do. Probably bite first, and listen later.

Leaving her hat in the car, she strolled into the saloon bar at the Jasper Creek Hotel. Looking around, she didn't see anyone she knew. All eyes were on her as she walked over to the bar, and slid onto a tall wooden stool. The barman leaned across to her.

"Hello, young lady. You'll be after the ladies lounge. Go through the glass door behind you, across the corridor. You can't miss it." He turned away, chatting with a group of men dressed in worn jeans and check shirts.

Their hats were sitting on the bar surrounded by glasses of beer.

Clearly wanting to see what she would do, the men watched her in the mirror behind the bar. Through a haze of indignation she heard their satisfied laughter, as if she were a minor problem taken care of by a pat on the head.

They couldn't squash her that easily. She said loudly, "Excuse me. I'd like a drink, please. Lemonade, if it's not too much trouble."

The laughter stopped abruptly, followed by an uneasy silence. The barman came to her and said sternly, "Look, love, you'll be more comfortable in the ladies lounge."

"Don't call me 'love', she snarled. "And I'm comfortable right here, you…" Mount Vesuvius was erupting when she felt herself caught around the waist by a pair of strong arms.

"Hey, Cassie," a deep voice gritted above her head. "What are you doing here?"

She was so stunned by Jack's sudden appearance that she was momentarily lost for words. "I'm getting a drink of lemonade."

"Me too. Let's go to the store across the street. There's a park close by. We can talk."

Jack stood aside as she glared at the man behind the bar and walked out the door. "Ronnie told me you were going up to Alcoota to dig up dinosaur bones," he said.

"I was up there. Now, I'm back." Cassie took a deep breath. "How could you do that to me, Jack. I was just about to give those Neanderthals a piece of my mind."

"It wouldn't have solved anything." Her eyes flashed with angry lights, Jack could see she wanted to hit him. He almost said, give it your best shot, but she would probably do it and hurt her hand.

"I was worried, Jack. Trouble follows you around."

Cassie stopped talking abruptly, afraid of what she might confess if she continued. "Where's Alicia?"

"Forget about her. She's not important. What were you worried about? Particularly?"

"You. I mean, that police operation is going to happen soon, isn't it? It's dangerous. I promised your mother that I would look out for you."

"Well, you've seen me. I'm okay. Tell her that. Also say that my foot is fully healed."

"What about the police? Are they here dressed as wranglers, waiting for something to happen? That's what the FBI would do. Lots of undercover agents would be hanging around." She peered around at the few people in the area, trying to pick which ones were police. They all looked like cattlemen or farmers. Not a cop among them. "Those guys in the bar weren't cops, were they? No hidden microphones or cameras? No guns."

"No. They were drinking too much. Police are around, somewhere though. Even I don't know who they are. Something will be happening soon, Cassie. I heard Silverton and his men are in town, staying at the pub. That's why you need to go, today if possible. I'll come to see you when it's all over. I'll tell you everything and we'll see where we go from there."

"I make my own decisions, Jack." Cassie didn't know why she was arguing with him. It wasn't as if she could do anything to help.

"Cassie, this is too critical to make rash decisions. If you won't do it for yourself, do it for me. Please."

When he looked at her that way, as if she was the most important thing in his universe, she took a mental step back. She would do anything for him. Even stay out of the way while he took care of business. Getting in the way was out of the question and pointless.

Surely this wasn't the OK Corral, where a shootout would occur. This was a civilized town, and nothing out of control would be allowed to happen. She had to let it go, and back away before the situation got out of control. Her just being there could change everything.

"All right. I'll go. But this is the last time I'm doing what I'm told."

Jack's shoulders relaxed with relief. "It's lunchtime now; you've got quite a way to go. I'll get you food and water from the store while you fill up with gas. Don't forget to get extra cans of fuel. Check the water in the SUV too. Have you got a spare radiator hose?"

"Of course. I've learnt the hard way to pack supplies." She looked into his worried hazel eyes and said, "I want to stay, Jack. I could be a look out for you." Cassie hated pleading but if it worked, she'd do it and think about it later.

"It's too dangerous." There was no compromise in his tone.

"No one knows about me. I'll look like a tourist."

"Someone does know about you. I found out Kev and Blue are still working for Silverton."

Cassie shuddered, remembering. "Do they know about Morialta Gorge? Or the cave where you keep your SUV?"

Jack looked grim. "Where I kept my SUV," he reminded her. "I hope not. Remember, I have my research notes stored in the cave. There's a safe. When Kev and Blue found you on that hilltop at Kalangadoo, they assumed we must be lovers."

Cassie smiled at the thought. She said, "So they do use their brains after all."

Jack looked grim. "They wanted to use you to get to me. I'd be forced to give them the location of the poppy. Then Silverton wouldn't have to pay for the information. He'd eliminate the middle man, that would be me."

"They don't know you very well do they, Jack?"

"I'd never let you be hurt because of me, Cassie. I care about you too much." Jack laughed. "Thank God they didn't know you either. That was quite a punch you gave Blue. And Kev wasn't real pleased to do a mudslide into the creek. They'd do anything to pay us back for what we did to them."

"What are we going to do, Jack? They sound as though they mean business, especially if you think of the profit they could get from selling drugs made from that plant. Doesn't matter that it's probably not addictive. It's still a drug, and worth money."

"That's true, Cassie. We have to believe the police know what they're doing. It's all set up for me to give Silverton the information. Police will be there ready to grab him."

"What can I do to help?"

"You can get into that pile of junk, and take off for Alice Springs. I have to deal with these men without you here. If you stay they'll use you as a lever to force me to do what they want. The police don't know about you, so they won't be able to keep you safe. It could be bad for all of us, especially if that drug gets onto the streets before being tested. Sometimes I wish I'd never discovered it, but then I think of the good it could do in the right hands."

Finally Cassie understood. The security of his diabolical crop of plants depended on her going away, before the sting operation began.

It was all clear to her now except for one thing. Would they be able to salvage something for themselves out of this mess?

She was about to ask him when he said urgently, "Cassie, get behind the tree. We've got company, but they haven't seen us yet. A couple of guys who work for Silverton are checking out my SUV. Try and get to your vehicle without being seen. They won't recognize it. You can get gas at that garage on the other side of town."

He handed her some cash. "Use this. Push your hair up into your hat so they don't see it. Red's not a common color for hair around here and they've probably been given your description by Blue and Kev."

"What about you, Jack?" Cassie put her hat on, hiding most of her hair.

"I'll be okay. The police are everywhere. Those two guys are headed this way. You need to get out of here. Now go!"

"Don't forget, Jack? Your mother knows my address in Melbourne. She has my phone number too. I'll stay in Australia until I hear from you."

"Don't worry, love, I'll find you, even if I have to cross the world to do it." He turned away, and as she hurried across the park under cover of the trees to climb into her rented SUV, she saw him sprinting towards his vehicle. It was much cleaner than hers, and she was sure it was faster too.

She watched helplessly as two men started running across the road and leaped into a car parked outside the pub. They left a cloud of dust as they sped down the road after Jack's disappearing vehicle, leaving a shaken girl at the wheel.

It was too much to take in. He had been forced to flee from the scene like a criminal, but he wasn't one. She finally believed he was one of the good guys and she was so proud of him even while she hated the mess he was in.

Surely something could be done about those men, she thought. After all, they were the ones who were trying to steal from Jack, not the other way around. Where were the police? She didn't see any farmer types leaping into cars, following them out of town. The town seemed as comatose in the sun as ever. Even the rust colored dog was still outside the pub, sleeping with his personal collection of wildlife. Cassie wondered if he'd even moved a muscle since she'd last been in town.

This whole situation was a nightmare; all she could do was go back to the city and wait. Or maybe there was another way? Cassie sat for a while and thought, finally deciding that since Silverton's two men had left she would stay the night at the hotel and leave in the morning. She tried not to worry about Jack as she gathered some things.

It was late afternoon by now, the hotel wasn't busy, and Cassie went inside to the reception desk, asking the girl behind the counter for a room. After checking in she took a quick shower, dressing again in cool tan shorts and apple green cotton blouse, her long red hair in a ponytail. Food was on her agenda. The pub dining room was quiet and cool; it was time to plan her next move.

Cassie ordered a salad sandwich, and as she ate, she thought, maybe it would be good to go to Alice Springs tomorrow, wait there a day or so, then come back. She decided to go out to her SUV, and check the water in the radiator, give the tires a kick. A little selective maintenance couldn't hurt.

As she passed the entrance to the saloon bar, Cassie looked in, drawing a sharp breath in alarm. Kevin O'Shannassy was sitting at a table, drinking with Gerald Silverton. They both turned as Blue Murphy came into view carrying a pitcher of beer.

Cassie swallowed hard as, heart pumping furiously; she backed away from the doorway. She heard a crash, a scrabbling of chairs, and knew they had seen her. She turned and ran, keeping a firm hold on her bag as she raced for her SUV, fishing the key out as she ran.

Where could she go? It was as Jack had said; if they caught her they could use her to force him to give them everything they wanted. The police operation would be cancelled out because they would have completed the transaction ahead of time, without the photographic or physical evidence necessary for a conviction. If there were no videos or tapes of his involvement, Silverton would win. Once again she had jeopardized everything because she didn't think ahead.

Moments later she threw her bag in the back seat and climbed behind the wheel. She prayed the car would start. It did. There was a spare can of gas in the trunk. The gas tank was half full, so she took off down the road, leaving a cloud of dust to cover her pursuers. Knowing they would be close behind, she took the nearest road out of town. It happened to be Dry Creek Road, which led to Morialta Gorge.

That's okay, she thought, putting her foot down hard on the accelerator, I'm committed to go this way now. That's all I can do. I only hope Jack managed to get away. Otherwise we'll both be screwed.

Of course there was always the hope that she could lose them, or they'd give up. No, she thought fatalistically, as she checked the rear vision mirror, seeing a dust cloud billowing behind. Blue and Kev will never give up. They have a score to settle.

After driving for what seemed like hours through low hills and scrubby trees, Cassie finally stopped at the entrance to the track leading into Morialta Gorge. The sun was still bright, the temperature relentless in her non-air-conditioned SUV. The track was still overgrown and unrecognizable, but she knew it now. She saw the dusty, flat, weed covered area where the flying doctor had landed, and where she had stood in the shade of a eucalypt, watching Jack fly away. It seemed like a lifetime ago.

As there was no sign of a vehicle following, she hoped that her pursers had given up, or at least had a flat tire. Maybe she'd get lucky? She turned the vehicle down the track, not worrying too much about scratches from tree branches. The SUV was so wrecked already; a few more ravages to the paintwork wouldn't even be noticed.

She climbed out, returning the branches to their previous position, before driving carefully along the track. This was no time for revving the engine; it was so prone to flooding it would probably choke and die. She'd never get it started again.

The overgrown track had many twists and turns, and rocks to maneuver around. Cassie slowed right down, concentrating on reaching the cave without breaking an axle. Suddenly, she came to a large gum tree blocking the track. It looked as if it had been dragged there deliberately. A chain saw was lying abandoned by the track.

Cassie climbed out of her car, looking around, hoping to see Jack. He wasn't visible, but this was the place he was to meet Silverton. That didn't mean there was no one else there. It just meant the thugs were keeping out of sight. Police would be hidden too, waiting for Silverton and his gang to show up. She hoped the police wouldn't grab her, thinking she was involved with Silverton. She needed to find Jack, and explain that she'd been seen and followed.

Getting the tree to move proved hopeless. All she did was break fingernails and strain muscles. What on earth was she going to do now? She was stuck and it was still a long way to the gorge. She would have to walk. At least this time she had proper boots on.

As she reached to get her bag out of the SUV, Cassie heard the sound of a vehicle pulling in behind her. Three doors opened and slammed shut. On a fast turn, she left everything and took off through the trees. Being caught was not on her agenda. She knew she was fitter than Blue and Kev, all it would take was a few clever moves and she could lose them. Of Silverton's fitness, she had no knowledge, except that he looked like a desk jockey. That didn't seem to matter; he was still coming up behind her.

She heard them crashing through the trees behind her, cursing, and picked up her pace. She had a slight advantage, being younger, skinnier and shorter, she could duck under branches, slide between boulders, and dressed in earth colors, she could blend in. Both Blue and Kev were smokers so they would have a hard time keeping up with her.

Five minutes later, a man appeared in front of her. About thirty five, dressed in tan pants and shirt, a cowboy hat and brown boots, his dark face hard and weathered, he stared at her, grim and dangerous in the way he stood. He held a rifle, clearly knowing how to use it. He didn't speak, simply gestured for her to be quiet as he looked around.

Must be a cop, she thought, relieved. About time one of them showed up.

Cassie was about to ask what he wanted her to do, when the man looked behind her, nodded, and moved quietly into the bush, heading towards the area she had just come from. She was uncertain what he expected of her. He hadn't actually said he was a policeman; he just looked like one, hard and sure of himself, taking control without uttering a word.

She turned around when she heard movement behind her. "Cassie. What the hell are you doing here?" Jack's voice was soft but lethal.

He was furious. Cassie couldn't blame him. After all he'd said about safety, and the reasons for her to stay out of the way, she'd blundered into the middle of the police operation, compromising the whole thing.

He said, "I thought you'd be on your way back to Alice Springs by now."

"I was. Something happened."

He pulled her into the shadow of a tree, making sure they could not be seen. Then he whispered, "Keep your voice down. You're being followed."

"I know. Blue and Kev were tracking me. Silverton was there too. He's getting his hands dirty today. Who was that man? Is he one of the under-cover cops?"

"Yeah. That's Dan Stuart. He's keeping an eye on Silverton and his mates.

At that moment, Dan came back. "You don't have to whisper," he said. "They've gone walkabout in the other direction. One of our guys is keeping an eye on them. He's snapping twigs to lead them on. The idiots think they're commandos."

Jack said, "Great. That gives us some time. Dan, this is Cassie Travis. She's on our side. Blue Murphy and Kevin O'Shannassy recognized her as a friend of mine and followed her. This was the only place she could think of to go."

Dan grinned, his teeth white, brown eyes gleaming. "Good job, Cassie. It's been a drag hanging around, waiting for something to happen. You stirred the pot well."

Cassie grinned back. "Thanks, I think."

Jack said, "We didn't expect them to follow you here, Cassie. When a call came through that you were coming along the track, and being followed, we put the tree across the road to discourage them from finding the cave. It was to keep the area secure. The police are coordinating their operation from there. I was supposed to meet Silverton tonight to hand over the research material. Now, it's all changed."

"Because of me," she stated flatly. "Sorry, Jack. I screwed up, again. When those two men followed you, I thought it would be okay to get a room at the pub, and stay overnight. Kev and Blue were there with Silverton. I had to get away fast when they chased me back to my car."

"Forget about it. Now I have to figure out what to do with you." He turned to Dan. "I'll take her to a safe area, Dan, then I'll come back and we'll work out how to get those guys. I'll hand over the goods, and you'll have your evidence. They won't know they're being watched and photographed.

"What about Cassie?" Dan asked

"I'll tell them I saw her, then she went back to her SUV." Jack grinned. "I could say she was furious at being followed by Kev and Blue, as well as sick of camping out with bush flies, and not having a proper bathroom. She decided to go back to the US, where it's civilized. We could hide her car to make them believe it."

Cassie laughed. "It's a good story. Unbelievable, but good."

Dan said, "Better, I'll drive the SUV away. I'll hide it, and then I'll double back. They'll never know the difference."

"I could wait at the cave," suggested Cassie, not

wanting to be left out of the equation. They seemed to have forgotten she was there.

"That's no good." Jack shook his head. "A bunch of cops have taken up residence in there and there's no room to swing a cat. I know another place just as good. Another small cave. It will be a long wait, Cassie, probably all night. I keep a sleeping bag and supplies there."

"I'll be bored out of my brain."

"I'll leave a flashlight, and a pack of cards for solitaire. You'll be okay, and you'll have privacy. It's got all the comforts of home. Well, I suppose that depends where you live."

"No spiders?"

"Not that I've noticed." Jack hadn't looked for arachnids. He didn't mention the bats. He didn't want to kill the idea of hiding in the cave before it got started.

Resigned to her fate, Cassie said, "Whatever. I just want to get this over. Lead on, Jack. Don't worry too much about the SUV, Dan. It's a heap. I don't think even the rental agency will miss it."

"That's no problem," said Dan. The two way radio on his belt crackled. He lifted it to his ear. "What's up?" After a moment he laughed, putting the unit away. He said, "The idiots have got themselves well and truly lost. I think they've found the river. Pity there's no crocs in this area."

Jack laughed. "There are tiger snakes instead." Cassie shuddered.

Dan said, "I'm off," and disappeared into the bush as silently as he had arrived.

Jack turned back to Cassie. "Good thing you're fast. If they'd caught you in Jasper Creek they could have held you for ransom." He flashed a grin, changing from a man on the edge to a man relieved beyond measure to have his woman safe. "You would have given them hell in captivity."

She grinned back. "They would have deserved it."

He was suddenly grim. "You should have gone straight away, Cassie. Damn it, I told you Silverton was in town."

"I didn't think he knew about me. Blue and Kev were with him, they gave me away. Anyway, I thought it was Silverton who followed you. I made a mistake. Sorry." She began to turn away, wishing she'd been more careful.

"Come here," he said huskily, pulling her into his arms. "You couldn't have known."

Cassie slipped her arms around his waist. Maybe he was glad to see her after all. She decided she would take Ronnie's advice, and listen with her heart.

"What happened to the men who followed you?" she asked, pulling away to look into his eyes.

Her heart started pumping madly when he placed a small kiss on the top of her head before saying, "I lost them in Jasper Creek. Hard to believe, it's such a small town. I've got friends with a house there. I parked in their garage, and then I waited a while before coming out here. I don't know where the men are now. Probably still in Jasper Creek, looking for me. Come on. Let's get out of here. We'll get you settled in that cave. I've got a spirit stove for a cup of tea."

"You got coffee?" He nodded.

She grinned. "That's what I need. I suppose you have to leave me there, but what are you going to do?" Her anxious query brought a smile to his face.

"We have some surprises planned for our visitors. I have to get back, make sure the fake information I'm handing over is ready. The real thing is too risky to take chances with."

"Be careful, Jack?"

"I'll be extra careful, I promise. I've got plans. Looking after you and making sure you don't get into any more trouble will be a priority."

"I was born in New York. I can look after myself, thanks very much."

Jack laughed at her cocky attitude. "I know you can, if you're on your own turf. You're in my territory now. I'll do the looking after." How he loved her. She was his perfect match, even if she didn't always follow his suggestions. He refused to call them orders.

Cassie smiled. "Okay. I'll allow that. So get to work and get back to me safely. I don't want to hang around in the cave too long."

Half an hour later, after climbing through rocks and trees, they came out at an area that she had not explored, previously regarding it as inaccessible. The path they were on was overgrown but Jack seemed to know it well.

He helped her climb over rocks, although she had no need of his assistance. She accepted the warm touch of his callused palm, knowing he would soon leave her alone, she didn't know for how long. It took all her willpower not to make him stop and hold her for a moment. She wished he could stay with her but knew he couldn't, not yet.

There was a sense of urgency about Jack as dusk approached, and she knew he was anxious to get back to the action. It was almost dark by the time they reached a rocky area hidden amongst tall gum trees and thick foliage. There was a rough wall of red sandstone that prevented them from going further. Jack brought out a small flashlight, moving aside some bushes, revealing a dark shadow in the base of the cliff. It was the entrance to a cave, a smaller area than the one he used as his field lab.

The gap looked narrow but he managed to squeeze in sideways. Cassie followed with room to spare, swallowing a natural aversion to dark, unfamiliar spaces. Caving was not her career of choice, preferring instead to dig above ground, but she'd do it if she had to. Sometimes taking chances was the only way to get what you wanted. Now was not the time to allow a phobia to rear its ugly head. There were too many ugly things rearing already, and as Cassie ran her hand over cold rock walls, she almost expected eight legs to crawl across her skin.

Jack took another flashlight from a rocky shelf just inside the entrance and turned it on, instantly relieving her anxiety. "This is yours," he said. "Don't drop it."

There were no spiders visible, no creatures of the night waiting to devour her, unless they were in those webs hanging from the roof. She shuddered, knowing she must conceal her fear. Jack needed to leave her, believing she was safe and reasonably happy. He needed to concentrate on his own problems.

The cave was larger than she had anticipated, allowing room to move around. Jack lit a hurricane lantern, light spread, giving a welcoming glow.

"There's canned food and other things you'll need plus bottles of drinking water. I left a sleeping bag in the corner, so make yourself comfortable. I wished I could stay with you, Cassie. It could be a while before I'm back. It's almost dark outside now and I don't think Silverton will attempt anything while it's black as pitch."

"Why not?"

"Too dangerous. They'll probably camp out near the river, and make their way to the lab in the early morning. I told them I'd be there, waiting. Surveillance cameras are already in place, so the police will be ready for them. In the meantime, keep this in mind, my darling."

He put his arms around her and kissed her, a long

drugging kiss that shook her down to her toes and beyond, creating a curl of heat in the center of her being.

For a few minutes she forgot about everything but him, and the way he made her feel. He was so tall and strong and exciting, the way his flesh moved against hers was magic. It was a cold shock when he abruptly moved away, saying huskily, "When I come back we'll continue this conversation, my love. It was just getting interesting, and I have some things I'd like to add to it." Then he was gone. She was left alone with emotions zinging out of control, a mind full of questions, none of which he was there to answer. There was also a sense of dread.

It promised to be a long and terrible night. She looked around, shining her flashlight around the rough rock walls. It was going to be sleepless as well. Arachnophobia was waiting just around the corner.

Twelve

"Cassie! Where the hell are you!" Jack's roar spread its vibrations through the cave with a resonance that could have shattered her eardrums, if she had been there. He came triumphantly in mid afternoon, the next day, to reclaim his woman, and found she'd gone, again. After the tension of the last few days, it was too much for him to accept. His frustration built until he shook with rage and a primal fear. "Cassie!"

He turned and stormed outside to see if she was anywhere around. Gone were his thoughts of the previous night and the outcome of his meeting with the drug traffickers. The police had wanted him to answer questions but all he could think of was his tormenting, irresistible woman, wondering where she had gone. She certainly had some lessons to learn and it would give him great pleasure to be her teacher.

He made complicated and detailed plans for what he would do to her when he found her, only to change them when he remembered that he loved her to distraction and what he really wanted was to hold her in his arms and never let her go.

Although Jack was a civilized man, living in a supposedly civilized society, most of his thoughts at the moment were primitive. He wanted to wrap Cassie's long hair around his hands and anchor her to him as he made love to her. When he caught up with her he intended to make her so exhausted that all she could do was lie quiet in his arms and recover, until the next time he wanted her, or she wanted him. She had put him through the fire and it was time she knew how that felt. He would be there to soothe her then, and she would stay by his side forever.

All that would come later. At the moment, she had vanished. He had to find her, but where the hell had she gone? It was quite a while before Jack returned to the hidden cave. He had searched everywhere in the immediate area, then gone further afield, but there was no sign of her, not even a footprint or a broken branch. None of the policemen who had come to this little sting party had seen her either.

Jack even climbed the cliff, looking out over the gorge, but the only things he saw were three unmarked police vehicles moving slowly along the track to the main road.

He was frantic. What if she was hurt somewhere, needing him? What if she'd fallen in the river, caught in one of the deep holes in the riverbed? He vowed he'd never forgive himself for letting her out of his sight, forgetting that she would have scorned his help, and done what she liked, regardless of whether he agreed or not. He only knew that the woman he loved had disappeared.

Going back inside the cave, he lit one of the hurricane lanterns and, looking around, saw signs of her occupation. She had obviously used one of the sleeping bags and eaten some food. He looked closer hoping to find a note or something to tell him where she'd gone, but all he found was an old blanket. It had been rolled up and used as a pillow. In the depths of the cave, it was cold. He hoped the flashlight battery had survived the night. She could have been afraid during the hours of darkness and gone looking for him. This was dangerous terrain, especially in the dark.

Cassie could be lost somewhere in the vast stretches of semi-desert that surrounded the gorge; they might have to call out Aboriginal trackers to find her. He wondered if Dan, the Aboriginal policeman, had left the area? He might be able to help.

Jack's imagination was working overtime. He decided to look a little closer to home before calling out the cavalry. After all, he told himself, Cassie wasn't a child. She was a strong, self-reliant woman who had been alone in the dark before, and survived.

Then he remembered her talking about caves. Something about dinosaurs, and joining a dig. He realized she might have gone exploring. The flashlight was gone. That was a clue.

He went deeper into the cave. Having previously thought it was only a medium size shelter, used by generations of Aborigines, he now realized he was mistaken. As he explored more thoroughly, he saw a shadow, which turned out to be the entrance to another much larger cave. It was a pity his research, and other concerns, had not freed him to explore. He might have saved a lot of time and heartache looking for Cassie.

There was a distinct possibility this was the way she had gone. She was always getting herself into hot water, venturing into unknown places. This time was probably no exception. Jack fervently hoped that among her preferred occupations was rock climbing. At least she'd know what to do in an unexplored cave. Panic spells disaster. He prayed that she'd be safe until he could get to her.

Eventually, he found his elusive quarry. It took a moment to adjust his flashlight, but when he did his heart leaped into his throat. He croaked, "Cassie. What…?"

She was standing, balanced on a ledge inside a wide, deep sinkhole. The flashlight was down near her feet, the light shining upwards. She didn't answer, or even look up.

Jack doubted she was even aware he was there; her

concentration was totally on another realm. He had the feeling that the hole went down a very long way. His fear was a living thing, eating away at his sanity.

How could she have climbed down into such a precarious spot without slipping and falling in, he wondered, shaking his head in disbelief? He refused to hazard a guess as to her reasons, or her method, of achieving this seemingly impossible objective. He knew only that she was in extreme danger. This was no time to question or berate her. They both needed to stay calm.

Jack put his hurricane lantern down, slowly edging closer to the sinkhole, trying not to dislodge the small pieces of limestone that scattered the area. She was looking at something in the depths. It would be disaster if he should startle her, so he said softly, "Cassie, sweetheart, I'm going to put my hands down to you and I want you to take hold firmly. Let me pull you out of there. Okay?"

"Jack, when did you get here? I've got something to show you." She looked up quickly and a small shower of stones fell, making Jack catch his breath in tortured suspense. What on earth was she doing, trying to kill herself, and him too, out of fear?

"Never mind that now, Cassie. Just do as I say. Okay?"

"But I don't want to come out yet!" she said, annoyed that he refused to listen as usual. It was like talking to a superior brick wall. "Why don't you be helpful? Go back to the other cave, get me that small spade and the nylon sleeping bag holder?"

"Cassie," he growled. "You're giving me a heart attack here."

"You're overreacting, Jack. I'm okay."

She turned on the ledge causing Jack to grind his teeth. He contemplated going back to the other cave to get a rope, but he just couldn't see himself leaving her there alone, even for a minute.

Jack knew he had to keep her focused or she would fall, destroying all his dreams for the future, as well as ending Cassie's life. An existence without her alive somewhere in the world was unthinkable, even if they weren't together.

"Sweetheart," he said, in a soft, gravelly voice, "I don't want you to fall. All I want is to get you out of there. It's not safe. Okay? Will you let me help you so I can breathe again?"

She looked up at him and grinned. "Oh, is that all?" She let go of the rock wall she had been holding on to then, without a sound, she simply disappeared.

Jack knew he was on the verge of a stroke. His blood pounded through his veins and exploded into his brain with the impact of a sledgehammer. His overwhelming horror and grief had him rushing to the edge, falling to his knees, scattering a cascade of stones into the sinkhole. Calling frantically as if the power of his voice alone could bring her back to him, he searched the darkness; his eyes glistening with unshed tears. Never in his life had he felt so lost, so alone.

"Cassie," he cried, over and over again, his heart bleeding like an open wound, his mind whirling in despair. Could such a terrible thing have really happened? Why did she let go like that? Did I do something to make her fall? Or Jump?

Thoughts ran through his mind in a kaleidoscope of emotions that would surely have destroyed him utterly if a feminine voice close behind him hadn't conversationally advised, "You'd better get away from the edge of that hole, Jack, it goes down forever."

All he could do was put his head down, gasping like a

stranded flounder, eyes shut tight, trying to breathe life into paralyzed limbs. He needed to recover from the biggest, most traumatic shock of his life. It had nearly killed him when he thought she had fallen down the hole. And now, here she was, grinning happily, large as life, her copper hair bouncing brightly in the torchlight. He shut his eyes and rolled over, lying flat on the ground, feeling like an old man, his limbs withered with the weight of years.

Cassie looked at Jack, and suddenly her grin disappeared. The furrows his tears had forged in his dusty cheeks were still visible. Cassie's heart lurched when she saw his distress. She sensed she was the cause, and cursed herself for whatever she had done.

It was all too much for Jack to handle. From living his life in an emotional vacuum, he had gone to feeling like a hysterical basket case. Logic had flown out the window. He wanted to shake the life out of Cassie Travis, as well as crush her in his arms and never let her go. Shaking won, for the moment.

Jumping to his feet, dislodging more rocks that fell into the depths without a sound, Jack Blackwood, research scientist, and previously a civilized man, lunged towards Cassie Travis with a roar of primitive rage. He wanted to grab her and shake her until she rattled, until she realized how much pain she had put him through.

For a moment she was shocked, then she looked beneath the anger and once again listened with her heart. She knew he wouldn't hurt her, couldn't hurt her. He loved her. She knew then the depths of his fear for her, and that his anger was his only outlet.

What had she done to cause him so much pain and anguish? Then she realized. It was the sinkhole. She'd been standing on the ledge, and he thought she had fallen in.

As his hands touched her, Jack felt his rage dissolve,

leaving a trembling explosive passion in it's wake. He pulled her fully into his arms, holding her tight, trying to make her part of him to keep her from danger, from the consequences of her own thoughtless actions.

He swallowed the lump in his throat, whispering hoarsely above her head, "Don't you ever do that to me again, Cassie Travis. Next time, I swear, I'll die of fright. You wouldn't want that on your conscience would you?"

He couldn't have stopped touching her, stroking her hair, holding her tight, even if his own life had depended upon it.

Her whisper of need was soft, but he heard it to the depths of his soul.

She said, "No, I don't want you to die of fright. If you did, I'd want to die too. Why don't we choose to live, together?"

Cassie put her arms around Jack and held on, unable to let go. When his lips met hers, it was like a raging fire. The only thing to do was go with it, to embrace it and absorb the heat. There was darkness all around them, and a silence broken only by sighs of pleasure, until Jack asked a question.

Their clothes had come adrift and were rapidly being discarded on the floor of the cave to create a place of soft landing. His voice was hoarse and full of need as he said, "Are you sure you're ready for this, Cassie? There's no turning back if we keep going."

"Jack," she snarled. "If you don't make love to me, right now, I'm going back down that sinkhole."

He had his answer and gave her his. There was only one way to go. Down, slowly and deliberately he lowered her to the floor. The clothes they had discarded were waiting for them as Jack showed her just how primitive he could be. She groaned as he stroked her waiting flesh, and heat raced through her blood as he entered her body, giving it everything he had, and receiving more in return. She wanted it to go on forever.

When the fire had been extinguished temporarily by exhaustion, Jack groaned and said, "We still didn't use any protection."

"You're all the protection I'll ever need." And she proved it by igniting his passion once again, and joining it with her own, her hands exploring and shaping her destiny. This was an unexplored landscape for her, and she didn't want to miss a thing. There might be dinosaurs underneath and around them, but they could wait. Jack and Cassie had until morning to find their way out of the maze they had created, and neither one was in any hurry.

Sensing he had been forever changed the day he had met Cassie, Jack knew a life with her was what he wanted above anything else in the world. All he had to do now was remind her every day that it was what she wanted too. Reluctantly, they picked up their dusty clothes from the floor and put them on. It was time to get back to the real world. Their bed had been made.

Cassie was all sweet compliance as she said gently, "I'm so sorry, Jack. I had no idea you thought I'd fall into the sinkhole. From where I was standing it was perfectly safe, provided you have good balance, which I have."

"Let's get out of here, then you can tell me how you managed to get off that ledge, and out of the hole, without me seeing you do it." He turned her towards the gap through which they had entered the cave, retrieving his lantern, but as he stepped forward, she pulled back suddenly, tugging on his arm.

"Wait, please. I want to show you what I found? It won't take long. I think you'll be as thrilled as I am. Come on!"

"I've just had the fright of my life, Cassie. I'm not sure

my heart is ready for any more surprises." She looked so crestfallen that he relented. "All right, love. We'll look. But after that I'm taking you out of here. I want to breathe fresh air and head back down to the camp. I've got a lot to tell you."

Cassie smiled with excitement. "Thanks, Jack. I've got a lot to tell you too." She took his hand, leading him to the back wall of the cave. There was a cleft in the rock. Her flashlight and his hurricane lamp gave plenty of light to see where they were going. It was tight, but he managed to squeeze into the narrow opening. It led down a slope into a huge cavern that was strewn with enormous animal bones. They didn't look like anything he had ever seen before, stunning him with the magnitude of her discovery.

"Well, Jack, what do you think?"

"I reckon a dog would be in seventh heaven."

Cassie grinned. "I can't be sure yet, but I think the bones are from the cretaceous period. They're too big to be an animal from these times." Her eyes were shining with excitement, and something like awe, as she and Jack inspected the skeleton. Jack was enthusiastic as he carefully helped Cassie pace the dimensions of the cave, brushing sand away from fine bones, seemingly forming a fan shape. It was hard to see much in the muted light, but what he saw was unbelievable.

"It's huge, Jack. I reckon it's about forty or fifty foot long. And look at that jawbone. It's magnificent. It must be a carnivore, look at the teeth." She looked at him with shining eyes. "I wonder if it's a kronosaurus."

"What's that when it's at home?"

"That's a type of plesiosaur that lived in the sea around Australia. It was the biggest marine reptile ever, a bit like I imagine the Loch Ness Monster looks, only with a shorter, thicker neck. Paleontologists everywhere will want to study it."

"It's incredible, Cassie. A fantastic discovery for you."

"For us, Jack. It's for us. If it weren't for you I'd be working myself to death, sifting through dry creek beds, and probably finding nothing. If this is what I think it is, it'll be of interest to the whole world. Scientists will flock here looking for more skeletons. They'll want to piece this one together, testing it to determine it's age, what it ate, how it lived day to day, if it swam in the sea or walked on land.

"I can't tell you how wonderful it feels to find something like this after all the time I've been searching. It's a dream come true."

"I can see that, Cassie. Your face is glowing." Jack looked around then, noticing that the cave had another fissure. He asked, "Have you been through there Cassie."

"Oh yes." She shrugged, offhand, not allowing herself to be distracted. "That leads to the ledge I was standing on in the sinkhole. My guess is that this whole area was once covered with water. This was probably a sea creature that lived here then. Look, there's some indication of earth movement, and fault lines in the walls of the cave. Maybe this area was a honeycomb of open caves and the animal was trapped inside when an earthquake occurred." She turned shining eyes to Jack. "It's like a natural map of the past Jack, with prehistoric signposts."

"We better get out of here now, Cassie. I share your enthusiasm but my stomach tells me it's way past lunchtime and I'm starved. Besides, I have some questions I need to ask and you have to be concentrating on me to give an answer. Okay?"

"Okay, Jack. I guess these bones have been here for such a long time now; I can leave them for a bit longer.

Besides, there might be CO2 gas down here. That stuff can kill you. It's better to let the experts have first crack at a cave."

As they came out into the sunshine outside the cave, Jack put his arm around Cassie and smiled down at her. "Let's head back to our camp. I can brew some tea, or coffee. We can talk."

"No police or bad guys still around Jack?"

"Not a one. We'll be all alone."

"You want to tell me what happened?"

"Not much to tell. The drug traffickers fell for the trap, hook, line and sinker. They turned up at the lab and I gave them what they wanted. It was a drug trafficker's show bag. The cops walked in and it was all over."

"What did Silverton do?"

"That was the best. He started foaming at the mouth, whining about entrapment. Cops ignored him. I think he thought he was going to a garden party. He wore his best suit. Even had on a tie. The rest of the crooks were a pushover, except for Kev. He tried to get his knife out of his ankle holster. Trouble was, he'd forgotten I took it from him. Then he tried to run. Dan tackled him. Blue howled, literally. He doesn't like handcuffs apparently. Says they rub his dermatitis."

Cassie grinned. "I like Dan. He goes for the throat. So what happens now?"

"They cool their heels in the lock-up for a while. Silverton is history, for now."

Cassie laughed. "Blue must be laughing."

Jack frowned. "How so?"

"He owes gambling debts to Silverton. Now he won't have to pay."

"Yeah. Unless Silverton walks free."

"Better hope he doesn't. It must have been nerve-racking for you, waiting alone in the lab for Silverton to turn up. Did he ever put that money in your account?"

"Yeah. I hope I earn some interest with it, while it's there. The public prosecutor will probably take it to pay the cost of this operation."

"That's fair."

"Yeah, it's fair," agreed Jack. "I don't want it. It's dirty money."

Cassie didn't want anything to do with drug money either.

"I don't think I'd want to be a cop," said Jack. "The slow pace would kill me."

"Good." Cassie snuggled into his arms. "I'd rather you helped me dig up dead dinosaurs. And I can help water your plants. It's a fair trade."

When they arrived back at camp they made lunch and ate in the shade of a huge river red gum, a layer of soft grass forming a welcome place to lie down and rest. Except that Jack had no intention of resting.

His whole life had been structured around other people and when he grew to adulthood his life had been structured around goals. He had achieved all that he had set out to achieve, but nothing meant a thing to him without someone special to share it with, without Cassie. She had become his talisman, his reason for being. He needed to tell her and, most of all, to show her.

Jack put his hand towards Cassie and stroked her shining copper hair, taking strands and drawing his fingers down, feeling the softness come alive and spring with a charge of static electricity. He felt her body reaching out to him, her eyes a golden glow of pure sensual desire. He was powerless to resist the allure of such yearning passion. He moved towards her as though on an invisible string. He had no resistance, nor did he want any. It was meant to be, he was hers and she was his, for all eternity.

He pushed her gently back on their bed of fragrant grasses and brushed her lips with his, searching for confirmation of her need.

In answer, she ran her hands up along his solid biceps to his wide shoulders, caressing the bare skin of his strong throat, smoothing her hands around to tug at the thick dark hair growing long at the back of his neck. He groaned, and she caught her breath, the sound of his arousal irresistible. She put both hands around his neck, pulling his head down to hers, kissing him, and enticing him to deepen his own pleasure in the kiss. It was sheer instinct when she moved her body closer to him, igniting a flame that was so hot it was like spontaneous combustion.

Cassie felt the heat in every part of her body, and knew by his response that he felt the same. The self-control that Jack had used with great effect in the past had spiraled out of control, and was just that, a thing of the past. He had drawn up the hem of her tee-shirt and was running his fevered hands over the soft flesh of her stomach when a strange whooping sound was heard close by, then a short sharp scream. It was like a horror movie, or a very bad comedy, depending on which way you looked at it.

Cassie was so startled at the intrusion that she shoved Jack away, disentangling their limbs in hurried dismay. It took her a moment, during which she was filled with extreme embarrassment, to realize that they were still alone.

No one had intruded upon their lover's hideaway, interrupting their first real taste of shared pleasure. No taunting marauder had prevented them from consummating the love they felt for each other, no human marauder that is. Jack was rolling on the ground under the tree, his sides shaking with almost silent laughter, his breathing a harsh intrusion in the stillness of the early evening. He said, "I think we were sprung."

Cassie said tartly, "This isn't that funny, Jack. I think you've got an extremely warped sense of humor. I nearly died of fright." She suddenly grinned at him, her own sense of the ridiculous coming out. "The joke's on you though. That owl brought me to my senses. Anyone could have come along and seen us."

"There's no-one out here but us," he said as he drew her back into his arms.

"I've decided to go back to Jasper Creek tonight and sleep in a real bed," she said. "No more of this lying on the ground, worrying about snakes and insects creeping into my sleeping bag. I want some comfort. And I want you." She looked at him solemnly and asked, "Are you going to come with me?"

Jack laughed. "No way."

Cassie scowled fiercely, hiding the hurt his words had caused. "Good, I reckon it was a mistake anyway. I want a man who'll be more than a one-time-only, here today, gone tomorrow kind of guy. I want someone who cares enough to stay around until the next morning and then some."

She turned on her heel and stormed away, intending to put plenty of space between them so he wouldn't see her tears. It was humiliating to be willing to give herself to a man for love, then find out he didn't really want her anyway, all he wanted was a woman, any woman. And it hurt like hell.

One minute she was walking towards her car, the next she was being lifted in the air and tossed over a brawny shoulder, the breath forced out of her lungs. "All right Cassie, you've had your say and now it's my turn. It's time to listen, instead of grabbing the wrong end of the stick, and taking off in a rage whenever you feel like it. I need a wife who'll be around for more than a day, one who'll be there in good times and bad. I want a wife who loves me so much she can't bear to leave me, no matter what." He stopped near the river and gently put her down.

"Are you asking me to marry you, Jack?" She could hardly breathe as she waited for his answer.

He shrugged and turned to look over the water. "Yeah, I reckon that's what I'm asking." He looked back at her over his shoulder. "Well, what do you say? Will you marry me? Will you stay with me for good? Here, or in the city, and some of the time in the US as well. Nevada sounds like my kind of place. Will you be my wife and have my children?" He grinned. "Will you share your plesiosaur with me?"

Cassie was overwhelmed. "I'll share everything with you." She moved over to him and stood by his side. "Tell me, why did you laugh when I suggested we go to Jasper Creek and stay at the hotel together. I thought it was a rather delicious idea."

He grinned, knowing by the way she stroked his arm that she was his. He bent and put his arms around her, holding her body close to his.

"Sweetheart, in a country town, especially in a country pub, everything that happens is public knowledge within seconds of it occurring."

"How do they know?"

"It's the bush telegraph. Sometimes it becomes public even before it occurs. I refuse to have an audience when I truly make love to you. I want it to be a very private occasion, just the two of us in a king size bed in a location known only to my wife and myself. A honeymoon in fact. A very private and deliciously long honeymoon."

"Oh, Jack. I love you so much. I want that too. And soon."

"Your wish is my command, my darling. But there is one thing."

Cassie's look told him she would give him anything he asked, without question. "What's that?"

"Well, I can put up with crows, galahs and parrots but none of those rotten kookaburras will be welcome at our hideaway. A man has to have some dignity."

"You make me feel incredibly uncivilized, Jack. Dignity is the last thing I'm thinking about." Cassie grinned up at him.

"Okay, forget the dignity. I'll just get my club. I left it back at the cave."

"Was that the bit of wood I tossed down the sinkhole? You didn't need it. I came willingly."

He grinned. "So did I, and it was the most incredible moment of my life."

Cassie laughed. "Mine too. Oh, Jack, I forgot to ask you about the poppy. I remember you found the one that you were looking for. That policeman, Dan, told me some more things about it, how much of a major find it was. How it could revolutionize pharmaceutical practices. Did you end up sending it back to the lab for testing?"

"Yeah. I sent it back with Dan. It's a beautiful plant. The color is about the same as your hair. A glorious red. That's why I love it. I named it the Cassiopeia Poppy."

Cassie was silent for a moment, her eyes moist, then she said, "Better be careful, darling. You could end up on the cover of Time Magazine. You'd be asked to do a photo shoot."

"That's no good. I'd have to be civilized and get my hair cut."

"And get a real job."

Laughing together, Jack and Cassie took a last stroll by the quiet river, arms wrapped around each other, lovers reveling in the gentle sounds of the outback as the sun slid down behind the cliffs in a blaze of glorious color. It would always be a place they loved, their own private paradise of dreams.

Also available this month from

Facing the Wind

Anne Harris

Is it safe for a small boy to play alone on the decks of a yacht? Erica Carmichael, social worker, does not think so. When she meets Greydon Mears, the boy's wild, unkempt father, her concern grows. As she sets out to investigate the child's welfare, she is unaware she is setting out on her own journey of self-discovery — a journey that will be rocked by doubt and fear, pummeled by deceit and betrayal. But by journey's end, will Erica learn to turn her back on the past and turn to the future instead? Can love give her the courage to finally face the wind?

Available next month from

Trust In Dreams

Jennifer Brassel

Elizabeth Reynolds is a dedicated doctor whose life is all mapped out. She knows what her future holds: hard work, career and a sensible match. Loveless and unexciting this may be, but it is safe - safe from love and the pain it causes. Only in her sleep does she dare to dream. Chris Grant is the most popular star on daytime television. His ideal woman is out there somewhere - a woman who can see past the fame and fortune and love him for himself. He is certain he has finally found the woman of his dreams and will do anything to keep her. But Elizabeth knows actors cannot be trusted, are never as they seem. Will she ever learn to trust in herself and follow her dreams?